SHIFTERS OF PADSTON
1

New SHERIFF in town

ANN EDWARDS

Characters and events portrayed are fictitious. Any similarity to real persons, living or dead is coincidental and not intended by the author. Places and incidents are either a product of the author's imagination or public domain.

Print ISBN Number – 979-8-227259-77-6

Electronic ISBN Number -979-8-27035-91-2

Cover Design – Lacuna Designs

PA Services – Lacuna Author Services

Editing Services – Weaver Way Author Services

Created with Atticus

Contents

To my Mom, thank you for being one of my best cheerleaders.
To my husband, thank you for all of your support.

Trigger Warnings

Please be advised, that this book is not for everyone.

If you proceed to read this, don't blame me and give me a bad review if you were warned and continue to read anyway.

This book contains the following:

Alpha Males

Dragons, Tigers, Wolves, Bears, and other various paranormal beings

Fated Mates

Bar-Room Brawls

Kidnapping

Open-door scenes

If all of this peaks your interest, please, turn the page.

If not, find something else to read, thank you.

Dig's
DINER
READERS WORLD
BOOKS

Chapter 1 - Chayce

The crackle of my radio breaks the silence in my truck.

"Sheriff..." Nora, our office secretary and dispatcher, calls out.

"Go ahead, Nora," I respond, trying to come across as neutral while keeping my fingers crossed that this call isn't one common for a Friday night in Padston, New York.

Our tiny town, located just over the Pennsylvania border, east of Lake Erie, is typically quiet. Most of the population is some type of paranormal and we stick to ourselves. The primary population of residents, both male and female, are unmated. A few humans live here, but most are mates, fully aware of our extra-special abilities.

"A call just came in from the Whiskey Genie." Nora's voice breaks through again, and my shoulders fall in exasperation.

"Son of a bitch," I mutter, tuning out part of the call.

"...Palmer and Dalton Cannon."

Flipping my lights on and doing a U-turn in the middle of the narrow street, I aim my truck toward the only bar in town.

"On my way, Nora," I acknowledge after keying the microphone. "Are any of my brothers around for backup?" Since missing most of the dispatch, I have no idea exactly what I am walking into.

"Yes, Sheriff. Brady is waiting for you on scene," Nora says, causing me to sigh in relief.

"Thanks, Nora, on my way," I say flatly.

The middle of winter in a remote mountain town has its own set of trials. More than just snow. With hunting season in full swing, it makes running in our other forms difficult. Caging up an animal for any length of time, regardless of sharing a human body, tempers flare easily.

Padston has a small number of unmated females. All of whom are highly protected. Unfortunately for me, those same protected females are usually the ones strumming up the trouble. It has yet to be determined if it's intentional, due to boredom, or accidental.

Coming to a stop in front of the Whiskey Genie, I take a deep breath before getting out of the truck. As soon as the door closes, I notice my brother Brady, who is also one of my deputies, standing on the sidewalk.

Brady gives me a chin lift in greeting as we turn to face the front of the building. Shouts can be heard coming from inside, even without my advanced hearing.

Yanking the door open in annoyance, the yelling only gets louder. I freeze in the doorway, accessing the situation. Brady almost runs into my back due to the abrupt stop.

"Keep your fucking paws off her!"

Hoyt Palmer yells at Dalton Cannon, pointing a finger into the man's chest to punctuate his words.

Roree Martin, Hoyt's cousin and one-third of the Martin triplets, stands behind him as he faces off against Dalton. She has a bored look on her face as she stares at her fingernails. Rhodee and Raelee, the other two of the trio, sip their drinks as they look on in fascination.

Scanning the room briefly, I notice the rest of the crowd pretty much doing the same thing as they enjoy tonight's show.

Focusing my attention back on the men in front of me, I notice Dalton's eyes flash yellow, indicating his wolf is very close to the surface. Brady steps toward Dalton as I approach Hoyt. Neither of them has detected our presence yet, too focused on each other. As soon as Hoyt realizes we are here, his shoulders sag. Spinning around, giving me his back, he immediately puts his hands behind him.

This, unfortunately, happens often enough that they all know the drill. The guilty party spends the night in jail, paying a hundred-dollar fine. In the morning, after cooler heads have prevailed, they go free. If they resist or break anything, the situation becomes altogether different.

A chorus of awws rings out as Brady and I escort our two troublemakers down the street to the jail. Their alphas will be called in the morning.

Once our overnight guests are settled, I head to my office and start my reports. Brady, bless his heart, sets a fresh cup of coffee on my desk before lowering himself into one of the chairs on the opposite side.

Looking up as I reach for the cup, his face is full of laughter. When he says nothing, his lips twitching, my curiosity gets the better of me.

"What's so funny?"

"You really did have tunnel vision back there, didn't you?" he asks, holding in his laughter.

Gulping down half the cup of coffee, I give him a minute to elaborate. My free hand spins in a circle, indicating that he get to the point.

"From what I can tell, they have started betting on the fights," he finally says, looking at me expectantly.

Shrugging one shoulder, I respond after finishing the rest of my coffee and tossing the paper cup in the garbage can under my desk.

"There isn't enough around here to keep them busy. Not yet, anyway. You know how it is. I need to pick my battles," I pause, making a mental note to check on the construction sites for both the casino and baseball field. "Besides, they always run the weekly football pools. I can't participate in one and condemn the other. If it becomes a problem, I will worry about it," I say dismissively, with a wave of my hand.

My desk phone rings, cutting off any retort Brady was going to make.

"Sheriff Galloway…" I say after picking up the receiver.

"Hey, Sheriff, it's Jorden D'Angelo."

Jorden is the wolf beta for his brother Crispin. Pack lands make up a large section of town, butting up to the woods.

"Hey, Jorden. What can I do for you?" I ask, despite already suspecting the reason.

"One of the pack members said you picked up Dalton Cannon tonight at the Genie," he says, as a statement as opposed to a question.

"As a matter of fact, I did. He was fighting with Hoyt Palmer. Something to do with Roree," I confirm.

He heaves out a heavy sigh before responding.

"Okay," Jorden says in response. His voice is a combination of resigned acceptance and annoyance. "Either myself or Crispin will be by in the morning to get him."

"Sounds good, Jorden..."

He cuts me off before I can end the call.

"While I have you on the phone," Jorden says cryptically, getting my full attention. "Crispin wanted me to mention...we have some foreign prints along the north edge of the pack lands." I sit up straighter in my chair, garnering Brady's attention at the movement. "We have increased the guards and patrols," he continues. "The scent was too stale to track, but we wanted to make sure you are in the loop."

Scrubbing a hand over my face, I notice Brady leaning forward in the chair before focusing my attention back on Jorden.

"Okay. I will have Adyr and Deakon take a look tomorrow," I tell him, making a note to myself as a reminder.

"Sounds good, Sheriff. We will keep you updated if anything changes," Jorden responds before disconnecting the call.

Brady stares at me expectantly. Falling back in my chair, my fingers drum absently on the edge of the desk.

"Not sure how much of that you heard"—pausing my thoughts for a moment—"the wolf pack found foreign prints, no scent, on the north edge of their land," I tell him, my head running through a lot of different scenarios.

Brady blows out a breath before he speaks, reading my mind.

"That can't be good...for any of us."

"No," I say vaguely as my eyes drift to the stack of resumes sitting on my desk. "The timing can't get much worse either," I finish.

Brady braces his elbows on his knees, clasping his hands together.

"Do you think these mysterious tracks are related to the new construction sites?" Brady asks, taking that exact thought right out of my head, again.

Blowing out a frustrated breath, the strumming of my fingers picks up, showing my irritation.

"I don't know," I finally answer.

Construction of the casino has been put on hold. The original builders ran into financial trouble and were forced to sell. The property is an eye-sore. A shell sits in the middle of a large mud pit.

My feelings on both projects are mixed. The tax revenue will help our small town. Our residents will make more money with the increased tourism. Some of us might find our mates in the process, but I am hesitant to hope.

All of those are positive things.

It's the potential increase of crime that comes along with larger groups of people we aren't prepared for. Needing to hire more deputies is urgent, as the four of us just won't be enough anymore.

Hopefully, our quaint little town stays that way, but I won't hold my breath.

Chapter 2 - Regina

"Gina! Let's go!"

My teeth grind in annoyance at the booming voice coming from down the hall.

Work sucked, traffic sucked, and now I have to put up with this bullshit?

Jaygon Jones, my boyfriend, for lack of a better term, is dragging me to some corporate dinner banquet.

Last year, he convinced me to go with him after only knowing each other for a week. It was not only boring as hell but also awkward as fuck. People kept asking the standard questions.

"How long have you been dating?"

"Where did you meet?"

"Do you think you are going to get married?"

Oh, and did I mention that Jaygon spent most of the evening bitching about my dress.

This year, he insisted on going dress shopping with me. Most of what he wanted me to wear was more appropriate for a call girl. Not that I am bashing their profession, but my taste is more conservative. I am no prude. There's nothing like a hard fuck against the wall, accompanied by some hair pulling, maybe some light spanking on occasion. Most girls are into that kind of stuff, even if they won't admit it out loud. However, when it comes to my wardrobe, my philosophy has always been to keep 'em guessing.

We spent three hours in the store arguing over what was appropriate. At twenty-eight years old, with a set of tits that would make Dolly Parton jealous, what he kept picking bordered on risqué. In the end, Jaygon picked one he liked, and we left. He didn't know that I went back to the store several days later, returning his choice and buying something more to my taste.

Shrugging off my apprehension at the pending argument, I take a deep breath and let it out slowly. He is already pissed. What's one more thing?

I square my shoulders, taking another deep breath as I brace for his temper tantrum as I step into the living room.

Jaygon spins around when he hears the clicking of my heels on the hardwood floor. His eyes take me in from head to toe, his jaw ticking. Mentally counting down, Jay doesn't disappoint...

Three...

Two...

One.

"What the fuck, Regina? Where is the dress we agreed on?" he yells in outrage, his hand flailing in my direction.

Putting my hands on my hips, I give Jay a matching dose of attitude.

"*We* didn't agree to anything," I start, waving my finger back and forth between us. "*You* picked out something that would make me look like a whore."

He starts to open his mouth, but I cut him off, holding my hand up to stop him.

"With tits this size, spaghetti straps and a bodycon design do not work." Smoothing my hand down the front of my lace cocktail dress, I continue, "These are people you work with. One would think that you would want me to present a more professional look and not the kind where I spend nights on my back."

Several emotions cross his face before he finally barks out a quick "Let's go. We're already late," stepping out the door of his apartment.

Rushing to catch up to him at the elevator, I prepare myself for a long night. Thankfully, there's going to be an open bar.

Dig's
DINER
READERS WORLD
CARDS
BOOKS

Chapter 3 - Chayce

"We flew over the entire town and surrounding woods. Neither of us saw anything that might be making those prints," Deakon informs me, frustration evident in his voice.

Deakon and Adyr are not only deputies but they are also my brothers. Along with Brady, the four of us are the highest on the food chain, especially in Padston. It's one of the reasons no one gives us any shit. Even in their shifted forms, they can't compete with a dragon.

I give Deakon and Adyr a nod in acknowledgment, heaving a frustrated sigh.

"All right," I tell them. "Let's make a report so it's on record. I drove by both construction sites last night and didn't see anything out of place. Maybe take a ride over to pack land and see if they can show us where they found the prints."

My thoughts drift through various ideas of where to start looking for whoever is trespassing on the wolf lands.

Coming out of my head, it takes me a moment to realize my brothers are staring at me, waiting patiently.

"Sorry. Deakon, you do the report. Adyr, you come with me. We will head over to see Crispin D'Angelo. I also want to do a more thorough inspection of the casino and baseball stadium."

Rising to my feet, I toss the resumes I was going through onto the desk. What's a few more hours of delay going to hurt?

I am struggling to find several candidates to interview. Not only do we need some deputies with experience, but knowledge of paranormals would be an added bonus.

Pocketing my phone and grabbing my keys, Adyr follows me outside without a word.

All of my brothers know that I am struggling with the hiring process. Why the mayor's office isn't handling this is a mystery.

Chapter 4 - Regina

Last night was a complete shit show. I have officially had enough of Jaygon Jones.

My phone died last night, so when I got home, I plugged it in to charge but didn't bother turning it on. It only delayed the inevitable. As soon as I did turn my phone on, the messages started flooding in. Jay started with the text messages. When they went unanswered, he started calling. Deciding that I was a glutton for punishment, I listened to the first few voicemails. Each message got more and more hostile. Not wanting to subject myself to more verbal abuse, I just deleted the rest.

Being Jaygon's arm candy for the night was one thing. Trying to pimp me out to his coworkers crossed a line. Under the guise of needing to use the ladies' room, I slipped out a side door and hopped in a cab, making my escape.

Now that I have had my coffee and time to analyze my dating situation, I decide that I need a break from everything. Pulling my suitcase out from under my bed, I start tossing clothes inside. Work is a non-issue since I can do it anywhere as long as there is an internet connection, but I do have to change my in-person meetings to video calls.

A quick clean out of the fridge and an email to the post office to hold my mail only leaves loading the car.

Stopping to fill the gas tank, cash from the ATM, and some snacks, I am on my way. Before pulling out of the parking lot, I hit the number for my older brother. He picks up after the third ring.

"Yes, my dear sister," Rafferty replies, sounding both sarcastic and humorous at the same time. "What can I help you with?"

"Just a courtesy call," I start, preparing myself for the third degree. "I am taking a road trip, leaving town for a while."

"What did he do? And where are you going?" Rafferty's brusque tone has me cringing briefly before a smile overtakes my face. Raff knows me well.

"As to where I am going, not sure yet. As far as the first question," I pause, knowing that Rafferty's temper is going to get the best of him. "Before I tell you, you need to promise not to go after him."

Rafferty is a sergeant in the police department. As soon as he finds out what Jay tried to do all hell is going to break loose. I can't have him putting his job in jeopardy over something this petty.

"Mother..." Raff starts before cutting off the rest of that phrase. "What did the prick do, Regina?" he grinds out. The use of my full name shows how truly pissed off he is.

Resigning myself to having to tell him, I launch into the details of my evening.

"Jay had the idea to pass me around to his colleagues last night," I say with a tired breath. "I left him there, catching a cab. He's been blowing up my phone all morning, getting meaner with each message."

Bracing myself for Raff's reaction, I am surprised when he heaves a heavy breath. His tone lacks the venom I expected, but I know better than to take his restraint for apathy.

"I am going to pay him a visit. No woman should be treated that way..."

Cutting Raff off before he gets into a long-winded rant, my voice is harsh at first. "Raff!" I pause to make sure I have his attention. "I am going to call him after we hang up. He isn't worth the hassle. He and I are D. O. N. E," I continue, spelling out the word to emphasize my point. "Once I decide to stop somewhere, I will text you and let you know the result of our conversation. Then you can decide what happens, deal?" My voice turns sticky-sweet at the end, knowing how it trips Rafferty's soft spot for me.

It takes him a moment to respond, no doubt weighing his options on whether to ignore me or not.

"Fine! Not that you are giving me many options. Jaygoff gets a reprieve, for now," Rafferty finally agrees, buying me a little bit of time to handle this myself.

Chuckling at his play on Jaygon's name, our conversation turns to other things. We speak a little more before ending the call.

Before my fingers move to call Emmalee, my best friend, Jay's name flashes on the caller ID.

Rolling my eyes, wanting to get this conversation over with, I accept the call. Jay doesn't give me a chance to say hello before he starts ranting at me.

"What the fuck, Regina? You just take off, leaving me holding my dick. I looked like a total asshole in front of all my coworkers when you bailed on me. Why did you leave?"

When Jay finally stops to take a breath, my voice is laced with venom.

"Jay, we are over," I say with a slight wobble in my voice. Pushing back the anger, I continue. "You paid me the biggest insult last night when you started acting like you were my pimp." I take a breath and deliver the final blow, "You will forget I exist and lose my phone number."

My hands are shaking in anger, but somehow, I manage to keep my voice even.

"You have always acted better than everyone else, Regina. I will not be humiliated list this, you frigid bitch!"

Jaygon is screaming at me now. Refusing to stoop to his level, my finger hits the button, ending the call. I make a mental note to block him later, knowing he won't let this go. Jaygon won't take my rejection lightly, which is part of the reason I am leaving town for a while.

Stopping at a red light, I shake my hands out, wiping them down my pants leg to dry them off. Twisting my neck quickly to the left and right, it cracks loudly.

Pushing thoughts of Jaygon from my mind, Emmalee is my next call. As soon as she answers, a big smile crosses my face.

"What up, bitch?" Her snarky yet cheerful tone brings a smile to my face, chasing away the ill feelings left behind from my conversation with Jaygon.

"Oh, you know...dealing with asshole men who think they own you. How about you?" My words have a bit of an edge to them that Emmalee picks up on immediately.

"Hold the fuck on," she orders. "What?" The single-word exclamation lets me know how pissed off she is on my behalf.

Once again, for her benefit, I run through the details of last night. By the time my story ends, Emma is ready to castrate Jay.

"Where are you running to now, then?" she asks with laughter in her voice, despite her irritation at my ex-boyfriend just a moment earlier.

"Don't act like you know me." My tone is light despite my anxiety.

Emmalee and I have been friends since junior high. Both she and my brother know me too well. When life gets too serious, I run.

"There is no destination in mind," I say flatly, causing her to chuckle.

"All right," she says with a sigh. "Let me know if you need to talk. Make sure you text me every once in a while so I know you haven't gone over a cliff or something." She says the last part with a giggle.

"Yeah, once I get to a hotel tonight, I get to let Rafferty off his leash It will make him happy. He was not the president of Jaygon's fan club," I tell her as if she wasn't vying for that spot.

"That would be fun to watch," she says, enjoying this too much.

"Yeah...all right, I am going to pay attention to the road. I will call you in a day or two to check in. Love you, babe," I tell her, meaning every word.

"Love you too, G. We'll chat soon. Be careful," she says before hanging up.

Starting a new audiobook, my thoughts get lost on the open road.

Dig's
DINER
READERS WORLD
BOOKS

Chapter 5 - Chayce

"Crispin, we made a report and I will add this to it. These tracks don't look familiar. It could be something drifted off the game lands, but no animal I know of makes these prints"—pausing to look down to the ground again—"it is really strange that there is no scent."

"I agree, Sheriff. We will stay on alert. With this approaching storm, it is debatable if the snow is going to help or hurt," Crispin says as he looks toward the heavy clouds of the approaching snowstorm.

"Yeah, town will be busy with everyone getting supplies before being contained. Just keep me posted if you find anything else," I tell him as I run a hand across the back of my neck in frustration.

Adyr went with the pack beta, Jorden, going east, while Crispin, the pack alpha, and I walked north. We took pictures along the way, trying to preserve the already distorted evidence.

"If your guards do find something, can you try and have them take pictures?" Crispin opens his mouth to protest my suggestion, but I keep talking. "I understand it's tough to do in wolf form, but it might give us a comparison or show something we might have missed today."

"We will figure something out," he says in response, with a slight nod in agreement.

Once Jorden and Adyr catch up with us we all shake hands before me and Adyr get into my truck and head back toward town.

"How bad do you think this storm is going to be?" Adyr asks me, changing the subject.

Peering at the darkening sky through the windshield, it takes a moment for me to answer.

"There is something in the wind that is making me uneasy. The four of us need to be diligent until this storm passes," I say off-handedly, hoping my brother doesn't scent the lie. If Adyr does, he says nothing about it.

Each of us gets lost in our thoughts as we pass first the casino project and then the baseball field. My words interrupt Adyr's thoughts.

"Message Brady and Deakon for me. You and I will go home to try and grab some sleep."

Running through my storm list, my thoughts are jumbled and chaotic. "Also, ask them to fill up all four trucks. Make sure we have supplies not only in the office but also the emergency kits."

Adyr immediately pulls out his phone, fingers flying quickly over the surface.

"That's done. What else?" he asks, going into protection mode.

"Have them check with the Morrises. If they need anything, we might need to get them help," I respond, mentally running through my to-do list for storm preparedness. This is the first major snowstorm this season.

The Morris family runs the local garage. They are tiger shifters who helped found our small town.

"We also need to check in with the Hamiltons," I tell him and then correct myself. "They are probably swamped. This storm is supposed to start around seven tonight."

Like the Morrises, the Hamiltons are one of the founding families. They own the only grocery store in town. Adyr's chuckle brings my attention back to him.

"Chayce, relax, brother. Everyone knows the drill," he says, stating the obvious.

My shoulders sag. "You're right. I do this to myself every year. Everyone here knows the drill. Worst case, they can defer to their animals." Pausing for a moment as we approach the sheriff's office.

Once the truck is parked, I turn to face Adyr before getting out. He pauses as my voice drops to almost a whisper.

"Something about this storm feels different. It is bothering me and I don't know why."

He pats my shoulder before placing his hand on the door handle.

"Don't stress yourself out. All you can do is prepare for the worst and hope for the best." Waving his hand in the air as he climbs out of my truck, he speaks with a chuckle. "I wouldn't worry too much. Most of the time, the weatherman is wrong. This is probably going to just blow over with a dusting."

Adyr leaves that statement hang in the air as he slams the door closed before heading to his own truck.

I really hope he didn't just jinx us.

Chapter 6 - Regina

"Recalculating…recalculating…"

The electronic, monotone voice of my GPS is grating on my already frayed nerves.

My audiobook got to a really good spot in the story, completely pulling me in. It wasn't until the snow started coming down in large, wet flakes that it occurred to me that I should have checked a weather report.

The GPS is supposed to be directing me to the closest hotel. The winding mountain road that I find myself on is ratcheting up my nerves, as the snow is hindering visibility. I turn down the radio after shutting off my book so that I can see better. It sounds dumb, but anyone who has driven in weather like this has done the same thing at least once.

The car has been in four-wheel drive for a while now. My speed is much slower than the posted speed limit. Having seen no other cars for over an hour, I keep the car close to what I think is the centerline.

Coming around a bend, a scream escapes me as, reflexively, my foot hits the brake pedal, causing the car to fishtail. A light gray wolf that had been in the road darts out of the way at the last minute.

Between the slick road and over-correcting my steering, the car continues to fishtail, and I lose control. Cursing the animal and my own bad luck, I brace myself as my car slides into the hillside with a jarring thump.

The airbags deploy, keeping me from hitting the steering wheel. Despite the airbag, my head bounces off the window…hard.

Touching my hand to my head, my fingers come away wet. Once the bags deflate some, I look through the windows, catching sight of the wolf staring at me. The human-like behavior has me shaking my head. Doing so causes my world to go dark.

Dig's
DINER
READERS WORLD
BOOKS

Chapter 7 - Chayce

Despite Adyr's optimism, the weatherman wasn't wrong. Unfortunately, he wasn't right either. This storm is so much worse than predicted.

Adyr and I relieved Brady and Deakon around five, so they had time to grab some sleep.

It's now eight o'clock, and we already have three inches of snow, with no sign of it stopping.

Since the four of us are dragons, we take care of snow removal. Being able to breathe fire helps save the town money.

Brady and Adyr are currently in the air, melting the snow on the roads as they fly around town when my phone rings.

"Sheriff Galloway..."

"Hey, Sheriff, it's Crispin D'Angelo."

"What can I help you with, Crispin?" While my tone is professional, apprehension fills me, waiting for his response. I have my hands full as it is with this storm and keeping the safety of the townsfolk in the forefront.

"One of my guards just reported in. An SUV lost control on the fifth turn on Padston Pass."

Pinching the bridge of my nose and curing under my breath, I push my irritation down, focusing on the important parts. Padston Pass is a steep road full of twists and turns that runs north and south. The road is treacherous on a good day. Most people know to avoid it in this kind of weather. It's also, typically, the last road we treat for snow removal.

"Was anyone hurt? How many are in the vehicle?" My questions come in rapid succession, purely in sheriff mode, not giving Crispin a chance to answer in between.

"There is one female," Crispin answers before his voice turns serious. "Madox smelled blood, and she wasn't moving," he says, causing me to cringe.

"Fuck!" I yell in frustration.

Taking a calming breath, I return to the conversation. "Thanks, Crispin. We will take it from here. Tell Madox 'thank you.'"

Closing my eyes, using the mental link to my brothers through our dragons, I reach out to Brady and Adyr.

"We have an accident on Padston Pass. The wolf guards report she wrecked in the fifth bend. Can you please clear the way? EMS is en route."

"Yes, *Chayce*," they respond, almost in unison.

Using my radio, I continue issuing orders.

"Deakon, keep an eye on the town. Nora, can you please call the Morris's garage? We need a tow truck up on Padston Pass."

"Yes, Sheriff," Nora responds.

"Chayce, I'll get Doc ready for incoming," Deakon says helpfully as I continue to run through emergency protocols. It's been a while since we have had an accident to handle.

Not bothering to respond to Deakon, I turn my truck toward Padston Pass. My thoughts wander to what the daft woman was going up there in this weather.

Chapter 8 - Regina

Squinting my eyes at the bright lights, it takes a moment for my brain to come online. Confused, the pounding in my head reminds me of what happened.

Wolf.

Accident.

Opening my eyes slowly, the red and blue flashing lights filter through the continually falling snow. On any other occasion, the spectacle might be mesmerizing. At the moment, not so much.

Loud voices reach my ears as I spot the outline of several large figures. Gingerly pushing the door open, I hesitate to step into the deep snow surrounding my car.

It takes another moment to realize that all conversation has stopped. Looking up, five men are staring at me.

One of the large men steps forward, crouching in front of me. In the darkness, it is difficult to make out his features despite all of the lights.

"Hello," the man says slowly. "My name is Chayce Galloway, sheriff of Padston. We received a report that you had an accident." He pauses, staring at me. It takes a second to collect myself and form a response.

The word "Wolf" is all I get out.

My head is pounding. Moving my hand up to touch the store spot, he stops me. Both of our gazes move to where our skin touches. It feels like static electricity is traveling up my arm, causing me to jolt. The sheriff quickly releases his hold on me, his eyes narrowing.

"You hit your head," he says, stating the obvious. "Our town doctor is waiting for you in his office." Pausing his words, he searches my face for something. "Do you know your name?"

My knee-jerk reaction is to say "Jessica Rabbit, but I refrain. "Regina...Regina Chaney."

A small smile appears on his face. The sheriff's eyes seem to glow from within, but I mentally shake off the prospect, discounting it for a play of the flashing lights.

"Okay, Regina. Let's get you into my truck so we can get you to see Doc." He holds his hand out, but I hesitate, causing his smile to fall.

Twisting back into the car to postpone the inevitable, I grab my phone, purse, and laptop bag. I also take a moment to gather my wits. I am fleeing from a relationship. The last thing I need to do is fall under the thrall of the beautiful man before me just because he is rescuing me from an accident.

"What about my car?" My brain is slow to catch up, focusing on the important matters. The sheriff, Chayce, nods his head toward the front of my car. It's only then I notice the yellow lights of the tow truck mixed in with the red and blue from his service vehicle and fire truck.

Bracing myself on the frame of the door, I get to my feet despite my balance being unsteady. Before it registers in my foggy head what is happening, the sheriff has me swooped up into his arms, bridal style. The surprise has me squeaking in shock and my arms reflexively wrap around his neck.

"We don't want you to slip and fall," he says in the way of explanation, his voice full of concern. "You are already dealing with a head injury."

Somehow, he manages to open the passenger door of his truck without jostling me too much.

"I can put your stuff in the back so you can be more comfortable if you wish," he offers, holding his hand out to take my bags.

"That's okay." I put my seatbelt on and set my things down on the floor under my feet. Chayce shuts the door, cutting off anything else I might have wanted to say.

The sheriff calls out to the other guys that were in the street before walking around the front of the truck and climbing in.

Dig's
DINER
READERS WORLD

Chapter 9 - Chayce

My dragon is riled, and it takes a lot of focus to get him to calm down before I get into my truck. Once he is under control, I climb into the cab.

Starting the truck and turning up the heat, I casually question the woman from the accident. "So, Ms. Chaney..."

"Please, Gina or Regina," she says softly. The huskiness of her voice has blood rushing to my cock.

"Okay, Regina. What happened out here tonight? Do you remember?"

Trying to remain focused on the task at hand, it is taking a lot to keep my dragon under control. He is huffing and pacing in my head as heat builds in my chest.

"I was trying to find a hotel. My GPS wasn't working right," she explains.

"Up here in the mountains, cell signals can be spotty," I inform her. "Why didn't you stop before this storm hit? There were weather alerts all over the radio." My tone is slightly accusatory at the end. My dragon's irritation pushes forward at the fact that she would put herself in danger for no good reason.

Regina looks down at her lap spinning her cell phone end over end like she needs to distract herself.

"I...I was...listening to an audiobook. I didn't know the storm was coming," she admits as a flush creeps over her cheeks in embarrassment.

Focusing on the road, my lips tip up on one side.

"Okay, so you didn't know about the storm. You were trying to find someplace to stay." Recapping what I know, it is difficult to keep the amusement from my voice before turning serious.

"How fast were you going when you wrecked?" The accusing tone is harsh to my own ears as Regina's spine stiffens.

It's my experience that people underestimate road conditions just because their vehicle has four-wheel drive.

"I wasn't going very fast at all," Regina snaps before softening her tone. "Being on unfamiliar roads in a storm this severe, I know better. This isn't my first rodeo when it comes to driving in the snow, Sheriff." She sneers the word sheriff like it tastes bitter on her tongue before pausing and muttering under her breath. Her tone becomes more defensive as she speaks as if I offended her somehow.

For the second time tonight, one word catches my attention. The first time, I ignored it.

"Wolf."

"That is the second time you have said that," I say aloud this time, calling her out to garner a reaction.

"There was one in the middle of the road," she explains, causing me to cringe. "I tried to avoid hitting it when the car started to fishtail." She takes a shuddering breath at the memory before continuing. "I overcorrected and just made things worse. The strangest part is when the car stopped after hitting the hillside…the wolf," Regina pauses again, getting herself under control, "It was still there…watching me."

Knowing the wolf was one of Crispin's guards, I let the question drop for now. We ride in silence into town as I make a mental note to chastise Madox for being in the middle of the road. Although, I might have to thank him instead.

Bringing the truck to a stop in front of Doc Russell's clinic, Regina lifts her head from the headrest, looking around.

"Where are we?" she asks quietly.

"This is Doctor Russell's clinic." My tone is slightly condescending since his name is on the building.

"No. The town, where are we?" Now it's her turn to sound condescending.

"Sorry. I assumed you knew." My attempt at an apology is lame to my own ears. "You are in Padston…New York…" My words trail off in fear of further sticking my foot in my mouth.

Watching Regina closely, she starts to nod and then stops with a wince.

"Come on, let's get you inside so Doc can look you over."

Getting out of the truck and moving around to the passenger side, I open the door to find Regina once again holding her belongings. As she moves to get out, she sways slightly. Catching her in my arms before she falls to the ground, heat blazes in my chest at the feel of her body pressed against mine as I sweep her up again and take her in to see Doc, unable to keep my hands off of her.

Chapter 10 - Regina

Something about this town doctor is off.

Throughout the entire exam, I have been trying to figure out what it is. He has been nothing but professional, so that isn't it. No, it is something else. The fog in my brain isn't helping.

"All right, Ms. Chaney," he says. "Everything looks okay. No concussions, but you do have a goose egg on your forehead," he says in a pleasant but wary tone.

Breathing out a sigh of relief, his words fade away. Now it's time to think about where I am going to stay and where my car is. I am thankful that I at least had the forethought to grab my purse and computer.

A business card getting pushed into my hand interrupts my thoughts. Heat floods my cheeks in embarrassment at getting caught not paying attention as he spoke.

"Call me if you start getting a headache or develop other symptoms," the doctor says as if my odd behavior is normal, pointing to the card in my hand.

"Thank you, Doctor," I say, slowly getting to my feet and putting my coat on.

Following the doctor into the office lobby, my steps falter, discovering the sheriff sitting there waiting, presumably for me.

"Thanks, Tavan," the sheriff says as he rises to his feet.

The doctor disappears, leaving the two of us alone as awkward silence hangs in the air.

"Can you..." I start at the same time the sheriff says.

"Where are..."

We both chuckle as I hold my hand out. "You first, please."

He clears his throat before speaking, "I was going to ask if you needed anything from your car." Something tells me that isn't what he was going to ask, but don't push the issue.

"Yeah, that is probably a good idea." My words trail off at the end, already feeling indebted to his kindness. "Uhm, do..."

"What do you need?" he asks, his words rushed, eager, almost as if he is trying to anticipate my question.

"A place to stay. Do you have a hotel or bed-and-breakfast around here?"

Chayce seems nervous all of a sudden. Before I can read too much into it, he answers my question.

"We don't really have anything here. Not yet, at least," he answers. The statement is a bit cryptic.

My shoulders sag as my mind races on where I can stay. If they don't have a hotel, they probably don't have a car service either. My mind is spinning when the sheriff's deep voice interrupts my thoughts.

"You can stay above the Whiskey Genie. The owner has an empty place upstairs. I already contacted Gypsy. She said you are welcome to stay as long as you need to."

Without realizing it, a burden of the unknown lifts off of my shoulder Look up, I find the sheriff is staring at me expectantly.

"Sorry!" I exclaim before lowering my volume to a normal speaking level. "Yes, that would be great, Sheriff Galloway," I continue with a stiff smile.

"Please," he says gently, "call me Chayce."

I nod in response, but he misses the gesture, having already turned toward the door. The sheriff, Chayce, steps into the frigid weather, holding the door open for me. A strong gust of bitter cold wind has my feet moving. My sneakers have me sliding on the slippery sidewalk. Before I end up in the snow, a strong arm wraps around my torso, keeping me upright.

"Come on, let's get you settled."

Dig's
DINER
READERS WORLD
CARDS
BOOKS

Chapter 11- Chayce

Having this woman, Regina, pressed against me is wreaking havoc with my dragon. Clearing my throat as fire burns in my chest, I guide her to my truck.

"Where are you heading that you ended up in our neck of the woods?" I ask, trying to keep my voice even and tone conversational.

The dome light from the truck shows a blush on Regina's cheeks as she climbs into the passenger seat.

Closing her in the cab, she gets a reprieve from answering until I follow suit and turn the key. Once the truck starts, I turn the heat up for Regina.

"Well..." she starts, her fingers twisting nervously. "I ran into a few things at home."

"Are you okay?" I ask as my words come out hurriedly. Immediately, my dragon starts puffing smoke from his nose and I hope that it isn't emitting from my own. From the way Regina answers questions cryptically and her stand-offish attitude, I don't want to scare her off, but fear she is in danger.

"Yes..." Again, she pauses, making me wonder why. "The law ended up getting involved."

Now, I am fully alert and even more on edge. The strange prints on the pack land, her presence in the middle of a bad storm. Regina is involved with the law. None of this is adding up or making sense.

Slowly pulling away from the curb, I head toward the auto garage.

Stopping at the front door of the building, Cobi Morris can be seen through the plate-glass windows behind the service desk. Regina hops from the truck before I can register the movement. Jumping out to catch up to her just as she reaches the door, I grab the handle before she can, slowly pulling it open to allow her to pass.

Regina glares in my direction before crossing the threshold. Her lips purse as if she is biting back a retort.

The bells on the door bounce against the glass, causing Cobi to raise her head. A soft smile is on her face as her gaze bounces between Regina and me.

"Hey, Sheriff. What can I do for you?" Cobi asks politely.

"Reg...I mean Mrs. Chaney's car was towed in from Padston Pass earlier."

Regina cuts me off. "It's Miss," she says, confusing me.

"Huh?"

She lets out a small huff of annoyance, speaking louder as if that will help with her explanation.

"You said I was Mrs., it's Miss. I am not married."

Cobi chuckles softly at our exchange, schooling her features when my gaze turns to her.

"Yes, Sheriff. Kyle and Daddy dropped it off and had to go on another call," Cobi confirms.

"We need to get *Miss* Chaney's luggage. She is staying in Gypsy's place above the Whiskey Genie."

Regina shoots a dirty look my way, but I ignore her.

"Oh, sure. Give me one minute. I'll be right back," Cobi says.

She grabs a set of keys from a small cabinet hanging on the wall and steps through a door to the right leading into the garage.

It isn't long before Cobi comes back carrying two large suitcases and a duffle bag. Stepping forward, I take them from her before Regina has a chance to move and address Regina. "Is there anything else you need from your car?"

"No, thank you," Regina answers curtly.

Turning to face Cobi dismissing me, Regina asks about getting her car fixed.

"Here is one of our business cards." Cobi pauses for a moment, picking a small card up off the counter. "Kyle or Daddy should be in tomorrow to help discuss repairs. Make sure you call first. With this storm, they might be running calls," she finishes.

Regina mutters a soft "Thank you" before tucking the card in the back pocket of her jeans. Her phone rings, the sound coming from her purse, but she ignores it. Reaching for her suitcases, I push in front of her grabbing both easily in one hand. She huffs out an annoyed breath, spinning on her heel and heading for the door.

Her phone rings again, and as soon as it stops, it starts ringing again.

"Please answer that. It's obviously important." My words are short, the noise setting my teeth on edge.

Regina climbs in the truck and starts digging through her purse in search of the annoying device. Placing the suitcases behind my seat, I notice Regina with her head tilted back, the ringing phone in her hand. Fed up with the noise, I grab it from her and swipe my finger across the surface.

"Hello," I say, earning an indigent glare from Regina while being greeted by silence from the other end.

"Where is Regina Chaney? Who is this?" an irate male voice says.

"This is Sheriff Galloway." Ignoring the question on Regina's whereabouts since she wasn't in a hurry to answer. "Who is this?"

"I am a sergeant with the Boston Police Department," he says curtly, catching me off guard. "Where is Regina Chaney?" the man says more forcefully.

My mind is spinning with questions as to why a police sergeant is ringing her phone off the hook. While distracted, Regina takes the opportunity to grab the phone from my hand.

"What, *Sergeant*?" Her tone is short as she puts special emphasis on the word sergeant, causing my brows to draw down in confusion.

"Well, unless you want to come to..." She pauses her conversation, looking at me. "Where did you say I am again?" she asks me. Shouting can be heard, but I can't understand what is being said.

Focusing back on Regina, my lips move on autopilot as my mind continues to make sense of all this. "Padston, New York."

"I'm in Padston, New York," she parrots into the phone.

"Well, my car is at the garage. So, unless you plan to come pick me up, I am going to be here for a while."

Regina's tone and lack of respect for law enforcement have my spine stiffening. There has to be a reason for it. Only hearing one side of the conversation makes me even more confused.

"Yeah, well, fuck you!" she yells into the phone.

The hostility in her voice has my head whipping in her direction.

"You know where I am. You also know I won't be going anywhere for a while, so if you want me back in Boston any time soon, you will have to come and get me."

With those parting words, she ends the call, shutting off her phone as well. Regina crosses her arms over her chest, throwing herself back into the seat of my truck.

"Drive, please," she snaps, forcing me into action.

Starting the truck and heading toward the Whiskey Genie, my thoughts war with each other. Should I ask?

Glancing at Regina before focusing back on the road, her gaze is focused on the passing scenery.

Maneuvering my truck through the alley, we come to a stop at the bar's backdoor. To the left is a set of stairs that lead to the apartments.

As I shut the truck off, Gypsy steps outside. Regina hops out and moves around to the front as I collect her luggage.

Trying to hide my apprehension, I quickly introduce the two women.

"Regina Chaney, this is Gypsy Jones. Gypsy, Regina."

Gypsy gives Regina an appraising look as she hands me the keys. The women exchange pleasantries as I climb the stairs, a suitcase in each hand and the duffle bag thrown over one shoulder.

Jostling the suitcases to one hand, I use my free hand to unlock the door. Placing the luggage just inside, I hasten to rejoin the ladies.

No sooner do I rejoin the women does the radio in my truck squawk.

"Sheriff Galloway, come in, please," Nora's voice floats through the air.

Leaning into the cab of the truck and grabbing the microphone, my words are clipped.

"Sheriff here, go ahead, Nora."

"Sheriff, Adyr needs you out near the den. Alpha Palmer called about some tracks." Nora does her best to hide her concern, but I can still detect it.

Casting a glance over my shoulder, unsure if Regina knows we are shifters, my breath releases in a heavy woosh. She is deep in conversation, giving no indication she caught the radio conversation.

"Tell them I am on my way," I tell Nora before setting the microphone down.

Turning to the women, my tone is soft. "Ladies, duty calls. Are you good here?"

They both nod in response and I waste no time climbing into my truck and pulling away.

Driving toward the bear's section of town, my mind spins. So many questions tumble one after another.

What is Regina Chaney running from?

What is she really doing in Padston?

Why is a sergeant from the Boston PD calling her?

Why did she snap at him like that?

Not realizing it, I have reached the den already. Looking around, it takes a few minutes to realize Padston Pass runs close to the edge of the bear's land.

We need to keep an eye on this woman while she is in town. My dragon's feelings about her will need to wait.

Chapter 12 - Regina

Gypsy and I hit it off pretty quickly. She brought me the best hamburger and fries, giving me time to get a hot shower and change my clothes.

Needing to get back to the bar, she left me alone. With a full belly and clean clothes, I get comfortable in bed, powering my phone back on to call Rafferty back. Ignoring the messages, my finger hits his number, and he picks up on the first ring.

"Jesus Christ, Regina, you are a fucking pain in my ass!" he yells before taking a deep breath and exhaling slowly. When he speaks again, his tone is softer. "What were you doing with the sheriff? Why did he answer your phone?" Immediately starting in with a barrage of questions, a soft smile graces my lips at his concern.

"I knew you were going to have kittens and didn't want to get into it in front of him." I pause. "Which happened anyway," I snark before launching into the tale of my accident and the wolf.

Now that Rafferty knows I am safe, he is laughing by the time my tale is over.

"So happy my distress brings you amusement," I retort, my words dripping with sarcasm.

"I need to go. Some of us have regular jobs and need to sleep," he says with a yawn. "Let me know if you need anything. We'll talk in a couple of days. Love you, brat!"

"Love you too. Be safe," I tell him before ending the call.

Not feeling up to talking more, as the stress of today's events hit me like a freight train, I shoot Emmalee a quick text.

Me: In Padston, NY.

Me: Going to bed. I'll call tomorrow.

Em: Okay, Love you, bitch.

Me: Love you, slut.

After plugging my phone in to charge, I climb back into bed. With everything that happened today, it doesn't take long for sleep to claim me.

Dig's
DINER
READERS WORLD
CARDS
BOOKS

Chapter 13 - Chayce

Sitting at my desk, trying to sort through the ever-growing pile of resumes, my mind bounces from one thing to another, unable to focus on the task at hand.

The snow hasn't stopped, and we have gotten about eighteen inches and it's still falling.

My brothers have taken turns sleeping. As for me, I haven't been to bed yet.

When I returned to the office after leaving the den, it was easy to confirm the prints matched the ones from the pack lands.

Taking a mouthful of coffee, my face puckers. Frowning at the cold fluid, I call forth some of my fire, blowing into the cup to heat it back up.

A chuckle from the doorway has my eyes darting up.

Deakon is leaning against the doorframe. My gaze narrows to the cardboard cup holder and paper bag in his hands.

He doesn't wait for an invitation. Entering my office, he sets the bag down in front of me. Pulling one of the cups from the holder, he sets it down next to the bag.

"Thank you," I say, gulping down half of the cup's contents.

Deakon grabs a cup for himself before sitting down across the desk from me.

"You need to get some sleep," he says, stating the obvious.

"I know," is my only response.

Opening the bag, there is a steak and egg bagel that I quickly start to devour. Letting out a soft moan around a mouthful of food, Deakon laughs again.

"The snow is starting to let up," he says but hesitates, which warns me that bad news is coming. Staring at him, Deakon rubs the back of his neck, collecting his thoughts.

"More snow is due later tonight," Deakon says, before pausing again and I wonder why he is giving me a weather report; he looks around the room, refusing to make eye contact.

"Just spit it the fuck out already!" I bark out, too tired to deal with bullshit.

"When I stopped this morning to grab this," he says, waving his hand around the desk, indicating the sandwich and coffee. "Guri Hamilton said they had a break-in last night."

My hand pauses halfway to my mouth. Tossing the remainder of the sandwich back onto the wrapper, I curse under my breath, scrubbing my hands over my face in frustration.

"Does he know what or how much was taken?" I question, as one more thing gets added to the list running rampant in my head.

Before Deakon can answer, my mind flips to Regina Chaney. The timing of her arrival is too coincidental.

Deakon is snapping his fingers in front of my face, trying to get my attention.

"Sorry," I mutter softly.

"Where did you go?" he asks, his voice full of concern.

"Run a full background check on Regina Chaney. Her hometown is Boston," I say, ignoring Deakon's question.

"Who the fuck is Regina Chaney?" he asks incredulously.

Launching into the story of the accident and ending with her conversation with the police sergeant, Deakon lets out a slow whistle.

"What is the name of the sergeant? Just give him a call and ask him," he says, stating the obvious once again.

Deakon stares at me like I hadn't already considered that. Sighing, I say as much. "He didn't give me his name before she grabbed the phone from my hand. I didn't hear his side of the conversation, which is strange. Regina never used his name either, only referring to him as Sergeant."

Deakon is staring at me, his jaw slack. Without warning, he starts laughing. He laughs so hard he falls out of the chair.

Giving him a droll look, I cross my arms over my chest, leaning back in my chair as he continues to roll on the floor.

Shutting down my computer and cleaning up my desk, Deakon finally controls himself.

"Get that report filed for the Hamiltons. Once that is finished, run that check on Ms. Chaney," I bark out, shrugging into my jacket.

"Where are you going?" he asks from the floor.

"Bed."

"What about the interviews for more deputies?" Deakon calls to my retreating form, stopping me in my tracks.

"You aren't going to believe this," I start, turning around to face my brother. Deakon wears an expectant look as he climbs to his feet. "I found a set of triplets." A grin crosses my face as I watch a myriad of expressions cross his face.

"Are they shifters?" he asks hopefully.

"The resumes don't state. I have a call to schedule a video interview. Their boss had nothing but high praise on their work," I tell him, confident we have good candidates lined up to interview. If I get lucky, we get the triplets, and I can focus on this trespasser turned thief in town.

"Why do they want to come here?" Deakon asks with a sneer.

I raise an eyebrow at his tone. He waves me off before I can question it.

"You know what I mean," he says dismissively. "No one willingly moves here."

Letting him squirm a minute, Deakon's shoulders sag when he realizes that I am busting his balls.

"I do. Not many people move here on purpose," I agree. Crossing the threshold of my office, moving to the door, I call out over my shoulder.

"Do me a favor. Go and check on the construction sites. If the Hamiltons had a break-in, we need to check for problems there too. I told the construction companies we could handle it."

"I'll go as soon as I write up that report for Guri," he says just before I push through the main doors.

Chapter 14 - Regina

The snow has finally stopped falling. My stomach rumbles, urging me out of the warm bed. My bladder gets in on the act, forcing me to get up. I shiver at the cold, compared to the warmth of the bed.

Doing what I need to do, I brush my teeth and hair, pulling it up into a ponytail. Dressing in my warmest clothes and stuffing my wallet and phone into my pockets, I decide to see what this town has to offer.

After descending the stairs, my head turns left and right, trying to decide which direction to go.

Opting to head right and pointing my feet in that direction, it is a bit of a surprise that there is next to no snow in the alley.

Clearing the corner of the building, what seems to be the town square comes into view. There is a small gazebo in the center of a roundabout.

The buildings lining the main street are either brick or stone. My heart hurts a little, missing my brother and my best friend. Both of them would fall in love with this quaint little town.

Shaking off my melancholy, my feet start moving. Looking in the windows of the various businesses displays people moving about their day.

Across the street, I spot a grocery store with a small café attached on one side. Quickly crossing the street, I suppress a moan as the scent of coffee hangs in the air. A throat clearing has my eyes popping open.

"Sorry," I say, as the heat of embarrassment floods my cheeks.

The older gentleman holding the door shoots me a wink before turning in the opposite direction. Making my way to get a cup of liquid nirvana, several people stop and stare at me.

Doing my best to ignore the stares, I order a large caramel latte and breakfast sandwich.

The girl behind the counter hands me my coffee, telling me to sit and that someone will bring my sandwich out as soon as it's ready.

Sitting down at a small table in the corner, I people-watch to pass the time. Pedestrians walk down the sidewalk, many without coats. Seeing them in nothing but a T-shirt makes me shiver. It takes several moments for me to notice a pattern, there aren't many women here.

The clink of ceramic against Formica moves my gaze to the inside of the store. My breakfast is in front of me. Before I can say thank you, the girl who dropped it off is gone. My jaw goes slack at the speed with which she disappears.

Gazing around the small café and the section of the grocery store, I can see, it becomes glaringly obvious, men are the predominate gender around here. Shaking off the confusing and somewhat disturbing thoughts running rampant in my head, I decide to be a little proactive.

Pulling the weather app up to check what the future holds, I suppress a groan when I see more snow is heading this way. My mind races on what to do next. I have my laptop, so working is no problem.

After finishing my breakfast, I decide to grab a few things for the apartment. There is a small kitchen to keep some groceries, alleviating the need to always go out.

Cleaning up after myself, I exit the café and grab a cart before roaming the aisles. Loading up on some junk food, soda, and coffee, I round the end of the aisle and accidentally run into another cart.

"Oh, I'm so..." My voice trails off as my gaze travels up the muscular chest, eventually meeting a pair of pale green eyes. A dusting of light stubble adorns the strong jawline. My fingers itch to run through the mop of shaggy, dark blond hair on top of his head.

"Sorry about that," he says with a knowing smirk.

My mouth opens and closes several times, but no words come out. A deep voice comes from behind me, dropping a virtual bucket of ice water on me and shaking me out of my stupor.

"Crispin, nice to see you," the semi-familiar voice is clipped, sending a chill down my spine.

The blond god in front of me is now grinning from ear to ear as his eyes bounce between me and the man behind me.

"Sheriff..." Crispin, the man in front of me, confirms my suspicion of the identity of the man behind me. His too-bright smile is making me nervous. After a silent standoff, Crispin and Chayce seem to have had a conversation, though neither of them uttered a word. Crispin gives a brief nod in my direction before walking away.

"Have a good day," he says over his shoulder, winking at me as he chuckles.

My spine straightens as I turn around, my hands on my hips.

"Can I help you, Sheriff?"

The anger is obvious in my tone. Chayce ignores my attitude, looking down his nose at me.

"Why are you here?" he clips, jaw ticking in annoyance.

Rearing my head back in shock at his question, my anger grows.

"Do I need your permission to buy some groceries?"

Chayce pinches the bridge of his nose at my question. I don't understand what his problem is. Speaking through clenched teeth, he bites off his words.

"I am not referring to the store. I mean, in town?"

My eyes narrow at him.

"Didn't we cover this last night?" I bite back, meeting his hostility with some of my own.

Raking my eyes over Chayce, I take advantage of seeing him in the fluorescent lighting, since I didn't pay attention in the doctor's clinic. His chocolate brown locks are messy, as if he can't quit running his hands through them. Chayce's eyes are a coffee color that seems to blaze from within if the light is right. A small scar at the corner of his mouth adds character to the sharp jawline and straight nose. He is tall, around six and a half feet, if I had to guess. And don't get me started on his body.

The man before me is hiding some serious muscle under his clothes. Great, now I am picturing him naked.

"When you are finished checking me out..." he says flatly, causing my cheeks to heat in embarrassment.

Refusing to give this guy the satisfaction of seeing me flustered, I square my shoulders and turn away from him. Placing my hands on the cart handle, I take two steps before speaking over my shoulder at him.

"Forget about me, Sheriff. I won't be in town any longer than necessary," I quip.

Turning the corner, out of sight from Chayce, I put a hand on my chest, hoping to calm my racing heart.

Quickly making my way through the store to finish my shopping, I manage to avoid crossing paths with Chayce again.

As soon as my sale is complete, my rapid pace has me back at the apartment and tucked inside in no time.

Why is this man affecting me so much?

Dig's
DINER
READERS WORLD

Chapter 15 - Chayce

Forget about me, Sheriff. I won't be in town any longer than necessary.

That phrase has been on repeat in my head since Regina walked away from me in the store.

When she left, tossing those words over her shoulder at me, it took everything I had to keep my dragon contained. The spitfire has no idea she is dealing with a predator. If she did, she wouldn't have turned her back on me.

Someone knew what they were doing, that mass of red hair serves as a warning label. Thoughts of getting my hands tangled in her locks has my chest warming.

Regina's dark green eyes remind me of the color of grass. The slight smattering of freckles across the bridge of her nose and the apples of her cheeks make me wonder where else she might have them.

Blood rushes to my cock at the thought of using my tongue to play connect the dots with the freckles covering Regina's body. The set of tits she has are something spectacular and I would love to get my hands on them.

Tossing the blankets off my body, my hand grips my achingly hard cock. Grabbing the bottle of lube from the nightstand, the snick of the lid fills the air as I pop it open. Dribbling a small dollop over the head of my cock, my breath hisses at the frigid liquid.

The coldness quickly fades as my hand coats my dick, making it easier to slide up and down my shaft.

Images of Regina float through my mind. Picturing her on her knees before me, my dick gliding between her plump lips. Using a fist full of hair, I control her movements. Drool drips from her chin as I forecast as much of my length down her throat, causing her to gag.

It isn't long before my orgasm hits. My cum paints my stomach and covers my hand. Lying here, my motions still as I catch my breath. Something about this woman is bothering me.

Shaking off the thought and rising to my feet, I start the shower to clean myself up. Once the water is hot, I step under the spray. Soaping myself up, more images of Regina flood my mind. Having her in the shower with me, her luscious globes soaped up under my hands as I play with her hard nipples. Already, my cock is throbbing again. Soaping my hand, I tug hard, chasing another release. Wanting to slide into Regina's body and watching her tits bounce with each thrust has me coming quickly, covering the shower wall.

Resting my forehead on the chilly tile helps cool me off some.

In the back of my mind, my dragon rises. His irritation is evident as he paces back and forth, smoke billowing from his nose. My chest heats. I learned not to ignore him long ago when he gets like this.

"Mine."

My head rears back, trying to understand what he is talking about.

"Mine...mate!"

Regina? Regina Chaney is my mate?

You have *got* to be kidding me.

Taking twice as long as necessary to get myself—and my dragon—under control, I finally step from the shower. The overwhelming need to hunt and mate Regina rides me hard. This is going to be a long day.

Chapter 16 - Regina

"Kyle, how long do you think it will take to fix my car?" I question, wanting to get my car fixed so I can be on my way. My phone is on speaker, allowing me to work on my computer.

"Well, Ms. Chaney..." Kyle says politely but hesitantly.

"Regina, please," I ask, cutting him off.

"Okay, Regina. We contacted your insurance company. They don't think the pictures we sent warrant the cost of the estimate. They are sending an adjuster to look at it." He pauses, and I know what Kyle says next won't make me happy. "With the snow we already have and another storm coming, it will be a few days before they get here."

Great!

"What does that mean?" I ask hesitantly, expecting more bad news.

"Until the insurance company approves the repairs, we can't order parts." Kyle pauses again, and my frustration builds. "Once we get them ordered," he continues. "It could still be a couple of weeks before it's finished."

Reigning in my temper due to my own ignorance, I respond.

"Okay. Thank you, Kyle. Please let me know if you need anything. And if you would please keep me updated, it would be appreciated," I tell him, trying to remain pleasant. None of this is his fault.

"Sure thing, Regina," he says before ending the call.

Flopping myself down on the couch, I let out a frustrated scream.

My phone rings, and I accept the call without looking at it and immediately regret it.

"Regina, where the fuck are you?" Jaygon's angry voice comes through so loud I have to pull the phone away from my ear.

Deciding to ignore his question, I ask one of my own.

"Why are you calling me? We are done," I tell him again.

"We are not over until I say we are," he spits out. "Get the fuck home, *now*!"

Heaving a sigh, trying not to let Jay bait me into an argument, I respond, keeping my voice as even as possible.

"Yeah," I say with a breathy sigh. "You make me want to get right on that, Jaygon. We are over, done, caput. Whatever term you want to use." Putting the phone on speaker, I head to the kitchen for a cup of coffee. "Our relationship was going nowhere. You made it abundantly clear when you tried to pimp me out." Taking a deep breath and twisting my fingers together to stop my hands from trembling, I continue, not letting Jaygon get a word in. "Lose my number and forget I exist."

Quickly ending the call and blocking Jaygon's number, my chest heaves as I try to calm down. My annoyance at the delay of my car repairs has me sending up a prayer of thanks to the big man upstairs. It emphasizes my belief that everything happens for a reason.

Taking my coffee into the living room, I sit down and call Rafferty. He picks up on the second ring.

"How's my baby sister doing?"

Pausing to clear my throat, knowing Raff's good mood is going to disappear as soon as I speak, I try to hide my emotions.

"It's okay. How are things at home?"

"What happened?" Rafferty asks, immediately on alert. The man knows me too well.

"Did you pay Jaygon a visit yet?" My hesitant tone puts him in full cop mode.

"Not yet," Rafferty snaps. "Work has been too busy. What did the fucktard do now?"

Ignoring Rafferty's angry tone, knowing it isn't aimed at me, I launch into recapping the conversation with Jay. By the time I am finished, Rafferty is irate.

"My partner and I will have a word with him," he pauses, taking a deep breath and blowing it out slowly, "It's a good thing you are gone. You might want to stay there for a while, at least until we know he isn't going to be a problem."

"I couldn't leave if I wanted to," I state flatly. "The garage said they have to wait for the insurance company to come look at my car. It is going to be a couple of weeks, at the earliest, before they can fix it."

Rafferty heaves a sigh of relief, surprising me.

"Good," he calls out, causing me to pull the phone away from my ear to make sure I am talking to my brother. "Having looked up that town, it seems like a decent place. Not much crime is on record," Raff says. "It's also in the middle of nowhere. Jaygon would be hard-pressed to find you."

My shoulders sag in relief as a muted voice comes through the line.

"We need to go. A call just came in. Don't worry about Jay. If he calls you again, let me know," Raff says hurriedly.

"I blocked his number, so it shouldn't be an issue," I tell him.

"Okay, G. Love you," Rafferty says, a little distracted.

"Love you too. Stay safe."

Rafferty ends the call without any acknowledgment.

Deciding that coffee isn't strong enough for me and needing a slight change in scenery, I change my clothes and make my way downstairs.

Dig's
DINER
READERS WORLD
BOOKS

Chapter 17 - Chayce

It has been quiet for a Saturday night. Brady, Deakon, Adyr, and I have been busy cleaning up the snow from the most recent storm.

My dragon stuck close to town, leaving the outskirts to my brothers.

Regina's scent has been mostly muted, letting me know she has remained indoors.

We have gotten more reports of thefts and mysterious prints all around town. Something still seems off on the timing between the current string of break-ins and Regina's arrival. The background check that Deakon ran came back clean, but that doesn't prove her innocence. She might just be that good that she hasn't gotten caught.

No sooner do I shift back to my human form and dress in my uniform before a call comes through, ruining my quiet night.

"Sheriff Galloway, come in, please." Nora's voice comes in, preceded by a squawk of the microphone.

"Go ahead, Nora..." I respond in acknowledgment.

My dragon, already on edge and trying to get me to claim Regina, pushes forward at Nora's words.

"We got a call from the Whiskey Genie. There is a fight in progress."

Whatever else Nora might have said gets lost as a red haze fills my vision. My dragon tries to take control, and as my claws extend from my hands, the dashboard ends up with large gashes cut into it.

Forcing my dragon back, I do a sharp U-turn in the street, flipping my lights and sirens on, driving like my life depends on it.

Pulling up at the Whiskey Genie, my tires screech as I slide to a stop. Leaving my truck blocking part of the street, I march to the front door. It surprises me to find all three of my brothers here and waiting for my arrival. The loud noises coming from inside the bar grab my attention from them.

Rushing through the door, my brothers hot on my heels, the sight before me has my body expanding. The seams on my shirt and pants start to tear as smoke billows from my nostrils.

Broken chairs, glass, and plates litter the floor. Tables are overturned with many patrons cowering behind them. Four men, oblivious to my presence, continue to wrestle and fight in the center of the room. Regina's scent is strong and it's laced with fear. My eyes scan the room and my dragon hits his limit.

Regina is cowering in the corner, hiding behind an overturned table. Her fear is palpable.

"ENOUGH!" My voice is deep and guttural, forcing more smoke to billow from my nose and mouth as my chest heaves.

An eerie silence fills the room as all movement stops. The only thing missing is the sound of a needle scratching across a record, like in the movies.

A heartbeat later, my brothers are moving toward the men lying on the floor.

Slowly, I approach a terrified Regina, glass crunching under my feet with each step.

When I reach down to move the table, she recoils. Tilting my head back on my shoulders, eyes closed, I take long, deep breaths, wrestling my dragon under control and forcing him back. It takes several minutes, but when my gaze returns to Regina, she is now on her feet. She has her arms wrapped around her torso, eyes wide.

"Are you..." My voice is still harsh, forcing me to clear my throat before speaking again. "Are you all right?"

Regina bobs her head, seeming unable to speak, possibly from shock. Holding my hand out to her, she looks between my face and my hand. Trying to remain calm and patient, she must see something as she slowly places her hand in mine.

Heat flares in my chest at the contact and my dragon settles with her proximity.

"Chayce…"

Spinning around at my name being spoken, I push Regina behind me in a defensive stance, blocking her from view.

Deakon steps back, his hands in the air, as his eyebrows hit his hairline. His eyes bounce back and forth between me and Regina, even though he can't see her.

When he speaks again, he is guarded, knowing my dragon is on edge.

"Brady and Adyr took Declan, Madox, Farel, and Tennyson to the jail. Why don't the two of you head over, and I will interview everyone here?"

Afraid to speak, I only nod in acknowledgment. Deakon steps out of the path to the door. Tucking Regina under my arm, Gypsy steps in, blocking my path.

Gypsy makes herself as large as possible despite her small stature. Standing with her arms crossed over her chest, she gives me an icy glare. Being over a foot shorter than me, I have to give her credit for showing concern for the woman tucked into my side.

"She didn't do anything wrong, Sheriff," Gypsy says sharply, using my title instead of my name.

"Mine." My eyes must flash as I speak as Gypsy immediately backs down, her eyes widening.

Deakon gently grips her elbow, pulling Gypsy off to the side so we can leave.

Escorting Regina out of the bar, I forgo taking my truck, leaving it to block the street. The lights are still flashing and the driver's side door is still open.

Keeping Regina close to my body, we walk down the sidewalk to my office and the jail. Urging her inside while I hold the door open, she hesitates, looking between me and the waiting room. Unsure of what she sees, Regina stiffens her spine just before crossing the threshold.

Guiding her to my office, I push her into one of the chairs facing the front of my desk.

I step back as soon as she is settled, my voice still rough.

"Get comfortable. I'll be back in a minute."

Closing the door behind me, knowing Regina is safe, I rush to our small locker room and change into a fresh uniform.

As I change clothes, my mind spins on what Regina might be thinking. If she didn't know, or at least suspect that we are paranormal, she sure as hell does now. The pending conversation isn't one I was prepared to have yet, but this is a rip-the-bandage-off situation. My dragon continues to pace, although he has settled down some, knowing that Regina is safe.

Securing my holster back in place, I splash some cold water on my face, only to catch steam rising off my skin in the mirror. Closing my eyes and taking several deep, cleansing breaths, I will my dragon to calm before we go in there and talk to Regina.

Placing my hand on the doorknob, I mutter under my breath. "Here goes nothing."

Chapter 18 - Regina

Numb.

That is how I feel right now. What started as a simple evening, having a couple of cocktails and listening to the jukebox, turned into something else.

For the past thirty or so minutes, my brain has been trying to sift through tonight's events.

Two guys—hot as fuck—got a little flirty. They weren't inappropriate, but I was guarded and not really interested. One guy wanted to dance. Then, the other one started to pressure me. The next thing I know, two different guys show up out of nowhere and are trying to defend me. In the blink of an eye, punches were getting thrown.

It looked like something from a Wild West movie. No one stepped in to try and break it up. Some grabbed their drinks, moving far out of the way. Others stayed where they were. I thought my eyes were playing tricks on me as it appeared that some of the guys had claws, and their arms were covered in fur.

When Chayce stepped in, followed by three other guys, my heart leapt from my chest. Fearing for their safety, I was frozen to the spot. My fear turned into shock as Chayce seemed to expand. The sound of splitting seams confirmed that something had been happening. When it appeared that he had smoke billowing from his nose and mouth, my suspicions were confirmed that someone slipped something into my drink. Though, I don't know how since I never left it unattended. That is the only thing that can explain the strange things that appear to be happening around me.

The door opening quickly has me jumping, my nerves still on edge.

"Sorry," the man says.

Turning to look, it's the blond guy from the grocery store. He slowly approaches me, his hand extended as he speaks.

"We weren't introduced yesterday. My name is Crispin D'Angelo," he says politely. Stress mars his otherwise beautiful face.

"Regina Chaney," I say in response, extending my arm in return to shake hands.

Crispin starts to speak when an angry voice sounds from the door. Crispin spins to face the speaker as I look around his large frame.

"What do you want Crispin?"

The anger in the room is smothering as the two men stare each other down.

Crispin ignores Chayce as he moves to sit in the empty seat next to me. A growl sounds from somewhere, and Crispin laughs out loud at the noise. Crispin leans back, elbows on the arms of the chair, as he steeples his fingers together.

Chayce moves in our direction. Instead of moving to sit behind his desk, he grips the arm of my chair, pulling me to the right and increasing the amount of space between Crispin and me. I yelp in surprise as my body sways with the sudden movement. Crispin laughs out loud at Chayce's action and bobs his head up and down as if the move confirmed something. Seeming satisfied by the large space between the two chairs, Chayce finally moves behind the desk, lowering himself into the chair.

"How can I help you, Crispin?" Chayce says, his tone all business.

"I heard what happened. I am here to get Madox and Tennyson out." Crispin responds as if his presence should be obvious.

"Sorry," Chayce says, shaking his head back and forth. His tone isn't very remorseful as he continues. "The four of them all but destroyed the inside of the bar. You know the rules," Chayce says flatly.

Crispin moves to speak, but before he can utter a word, two more men barge into the office without knocking. Chayce pinches the bridge of his nose, muttering under his breath about catching a break. The men move closer to us without waiting for an invitation. Both of them stand behind Crispin and me, arms crossed over their chests.

"Guri, Arek, please, come in," Chayce says in total sarcasm.

Both men have their gazes focused on me. Another growl can be heard, and Crispin starts laughing so hard that he falls out of the chair. The newcomers look between Chayce and Crispin, confusion evident on their faces.

The taller of the two men—with brown, curly hair—gets a large grin on his face as if he is privy to the joke. A moment later, he holds his hand out to me to shake.

"Arek Palmer, it's a pleasure to meet you..." His voice trails off as he waits for me to provide my name. Chayce decides to answer for me.

"Not interested," he growls out.

My head whips in his direction, eyebrows furrowed.

"I don't need you to answer for me," I snap at Chayce before turning toward Arek. Taking Arek's hand to shake and pasting a megawatt smile on my face, he gets his answer.

"Regina Chaney, It's nice to meet you."

My gaze falls to the other man and he steps forward as another growl fills the room. All of us ignore it as he takes my hand, kissing the back of it softly as he introduces himself.

"Guri Hamilton."

Before I know what is happening, Chayce has me pulled from the chair and settles me in his lap, putting the desk between me and the other men. Guri and Arek join Crispin in gales of laughter. I try to get up, but Chayce's arms wrap around my body, holding me in place. Heavy footfalls can be heard before the three men who accompanied Chayce into the bar stumble through the doorway.

All three men look on in stunned silence at the scene before them. Unsure what expression is on my face, but one of the steps forward, speaking softly.

"Chayce, you need to settle down. You are scaring her," he says with a nod in my direction.

The arms wrapped around my body loosen slightly, but I still can't get up. The three men move to take positions on each side of the desk. As they do, Chayce relaxes a little more. One of the men—deputies, I assume by their uniforms—speaks. It's a different one than the one who told Chayce to relax.

"Gentlemen. You know what is going on here," he says with a wave in mine and Chayce's direction. "How can we help you?"

His words are a bit cryptic to me, but the three men in front of us seem to know what is happening and they sober almost immediately. With all traces of humor gone, each man has a humbled look on their face.

Guri speaks first, his hand over his heart as he gives a slight bow.

"My apologies," Guri says, eyes focused on Chayce.

Arek and Crispin mutter apologies as well. The first deputy speaks, leaving Chayce and me in an awkward state.

"Gentlemen, what can you do for you? Obviously, the sheriff needs to hurry this along." The urgency in the man's voice is confusing.

"I wanted to find out what happened and pay what is necessary to get Farel released," Guri says, all business-like now.

Arek and Crispin both nod, muttering a "me too."

"Well, gentlemen. We have not yet had a chance to process the various reports of tonight's brawl. You know that it is required for each man to spend the night to cool off," the deputy pauses. "There is also the matter of the destruction of property. The Whiskey Genie has a lot of damage. This needs to go before the judge. You know how this works," he says again.

All three men mutter expletives.

"We have pictures of the aftermath. If you would like to take a look at them?" the deputy states with a raised eyebrow.

Chayce chimes in and my spine stiffens as his words sink in.

"I will be making a case against all of them," he says flatly. All six men snap their heads in his direction as Chayce continues to speak. "She was there," he says, nodding in my direction. "Regina was in danger and frightened."

The color drains from each man's face.

Still confused as to what exactly is happening, my eyes bounce between each man. Whatever Chayce means has these men cowering. Why he has a sudden change of heart about me is unnerving.

Not sure who says it, but a muttered "Looks like there's a new sheriff in town," has Chayce's body stiffening underneath me.

Dig's
DINER
READERS WORLD
CARDS
BOOKS

Chapter 19 - Chayce

"Brady, Deakon, Adyr, can you please escort these men from my office, closing the door behind you?"

While my words get phrased as a question, it is anything but. With so many unmated males in the room with my frightened mate, it has my dragon on edge. As soon as I finish my request, all six men flee the room like their asses are on fire.

Regina squirms in my lap, trying to get up again. My dick gets hard, having her pert ass rubbing against it. Reluctantly releasing my hold, once the room is empty, she stands, moving back to the other side of the desk. We stare at each other, not saying a word, for several tense minutes. Finally, she breaks the silence.

"Can you…uhm, please explain what happened tonight?" Regina's voice wobbles, the events of the evening obviously getting to her.

Leaning forward, placing my forearms on the desk, and clasping my hands together, I start to explain, assuming she isn't just referring to the bar fight.

"What do you know of paranormals?" I question with bated breath.

My words hang in the air as a wide range of emotions flick over Regina's face. Deciding to wait her out, we sit in silence. She opens and closes her mouth several times while lifting a finger to point at me. Her shoulders slump as she seems to come to an unknown conclusion.

"Is that what I saw tonight?" she asks in a near whisper.

Her timid tone has me on edge as if her fear is returning. Springing from my chair, I race around the desk. Kneeling in front of her, I take one of her hands between both of mine.

"I am not sure what you saw or what happened before my arrival at the Whiskey Genie. The fact that you were in danger and frightened falls on my shoulders," I say, regret for not being by her side obvious in my voice.

"If you weren't there, how could what happened be your fault?" she asks.

"You are my mate," I hold up my hand to stop her as she opens her mouth to speak, "As your mate and the sheriff, it is up to me to keep you safe," I explain.

"Wha...what is a mate?" Regina asks hesitantly.

"Every paranormal gets one person to spend their long life with. That person is made just for us, our other half. Some people refer to them as soul mates. For a paranormal, it is much more than that. We have just shortened the vernacular," I tell her in a pleading fashion, wishing her to understand and accept this.

"And you think that I"—she starts, putting a finger to her chest—"am your...mate?" Regina questions, stumbling over the word mate.

Before either of us can say anything else, the shrill ringing of her phone interrupts the conversation. Regina pulls her phone from the back pocket of her jeans. Her eyes flick between the screen and my face when she sees who is calling. Answering the call, I can feel her body tense.

"Yeah," she says after swiping her finger across the screen.

"G, just calling to check in," the male voice says through the phone. The abbreviated version of her name tells me this is someone very close to her.

"Still in one piece and haven't burned the town down yet," she jokes, causing my spine to stiffen due to the circumstances around town.

The man sighs heavily. "Can you talk to that sheriff?" he asks her, drawing my full attention to the conversation. "See if he can keep his eyes open. Jay is a threat." My dragon is on full alert at his statement, causing smoke to come out of my nose. "The chance of him finding you is slim, but not something I want to take a chance on." His concerned tone confuses me.

Regina's body sags as her eyes connect with mine, an unreadable look on her face.

"Yeah," she says sarcastically. "Updating the sheriff won't be an issue," she says flatly, holding my gaze.

"All right, as soon as I get a chance to talk to Jay, I will let you know. Stay alert, and stay safe," he warns. "Love you," he finishes, causing me to bristle. Who is this man? What does he mean to Regina? What is their relationship?

My dragon wants to hunt this man down as he considers him a threat to our mating.

Regina mutters a soft "Love you too," but the man is no longer on the line.

It is taking everything I have to keep my dragon under control. The fact that she could be in danger is one reason. Regina expressing her love to another man is another. Dropping her hand and rising to my feet, I pace around my office. Having had enough silence and wanting, no needing more information, I do my best to keep my voice level. It doesn't work very well—my jealousy is evident.

"You have a man in your life?" I snap.

"Hmm, oh, yeah...Rafferty," she says distractedly.

"Have you been together long?" I question, unable to help myself. "And who is this, Jay?" My anger is obvious in my tone.

Waiting for Regina to answer my questions, it shocks me when she starts laughing. My feet freeze in place as I turn to face her. Tears stream down her cheeks, she is laughing so hard.

"Raff...is...my...my..." Each word is said through her laughter, making it difficult to form complete sentences. My dragon is pacing frantically as I try to keep him calm. Regina's laughter is not helping the situation. When she finally said the last word, I scrub my hand over my face at my own stupid jealousy. "Brother."

The door to my office opens, distracting me from the current conversation. Deakon is peering through the small opening with an eyebrow raised in question due to Regina's laughter. Waving him in, Brady and Adyr follow immediately behind him. All three of my brothers have their brows raised to the ceiling.

Ignoring them all, I pull the chair Crispin had been sitting in earlier up next to her.

"Let's put a pin in the conversation you just had with Rafferty for a moment," I say, more forcefully than necessary. "I would like to introduce you to my brothers," I tack on, softening my tone.

Regina takes a moment to compose herself, wiping the tears from her eyes and cheeks as her laughter dwindles to giggles before ending altogether. Turning around in her seat she gives each of my brothers an assessing look.

"The one on the left is Adyr," I say as he gives Regina a nod in acknowledgment. "The one in the middle is Brady and the one on the right is Deakon." Brady and Deakon copy Adyr, repeating a nod to Regina as their name is said. "Brothers, this is Regina Chaney, my mate," I explain in the way of introduction, making our bond officially public.

Deakon's head whips in my direction when I say her name. Giving him a shake of the head, he gives the barest of nods in acknowledgment. The look in his eye tells me that we will be discussing this later.

"What did your parents do, go down the alphabet when they picked your names?" Regina says with a chuckle as she points to each of us.

We all freeze, looking at each other in shock. All of our lives, we never made the connection. She looks to Adyr, addressing him first.

"Are you the oldest?" Regina asks, causing Adyr's cheeks to flame in embarrassment. Looking over her shoulder, Regina asks, "Does that make you number three?"

Giving her a slight nod in affirmation, she starts to giggle. What she doesn't understand is that we had a sister, Evelyn. She died at the same time as our parents in a car accident. Clearing my throat to break the sudden silence in the room, my focus returns to the conversation with her brother.

"You have a brother, Raff, you said his name is?"

"Rafferty," she clarifies. "He is ten years older than me. When our parents died, he took over raising me." Emotion causes her voice to rasp. “We are very close,” she adds as her voice trails off.

“Our parents and sister have passed away as well,” I say in a near whisper, letting her know that I understand her pain.

Regina’s head pops up, and she starts looking between the four of us. It is obvious the question she wants to ask, but courtesy has her holding her tongue. Brady answers her unspoken question.

“Our sister’s name was Evelyn,” he says flatly, as his lips tip up on one side. Since Regina made the connection about our names, it is something to smile about.

Clearing my throat in an attempt to steer the conversation back to her phone call, I ask, with a serious tone. “Back to the conversation with Rafferty, what and who is he talking about?” My brothers pick up on the tension my dragon is putting off. While I might be the third born, I am the alpha of our family.

Regina takes a deep breath, letting it out slowly as she launches into the tale of this Jay, or Jaygon. My dragon is pacing, smoke pouring from his nostrils, causing it to leak from my nose and mouth. It is difficult to notice, but Regina doesn’t comment about it. Her reaction, or lack thereof, regarding being my mate has been pushed to the back burner. Regina’s safety is at the forefront.

“Rafferty and his partner said they would stop by and have a chat with Jay after he threatened me. Raff wants me to stay put, not that I have a choice with my car being wrecked,” she says this with an air of casualness as if her safety is in jeopardy on a regular basis.

“Partner?” Deakon asks, confused by the statement. “Life partner?” he asks, trying to clarify. If her brother and his “partner” go up against a guy who is possibly violent, they are merely putting themselves at risk.

Regina’s chuckle and shaking of her head refocus my concern away from Rafferty. Looking over her shoulder at me, her cheeks flush.

“No, he...he is...a sergeant with the Boston PD,” she says between laughs. Her face scrunches in disgust as it takes me a few minutes to understand her reaction.

"*He* is the sergeant you were arguing with the other night?" I ask incredulously.

Tossing my head back to look at the ceiling, I take a minute to get myself under control. When my brothers start laughing, my head snaps up as I glare at all of them. Their laughter becomes so raucous that they lean against each other in order to remain standing.

Assholes.

Chapter 20 - Regina

Watching the four brothers interact has me missing Rafferty. Seeing them give each other shit brings a soft smile to my face. The three brothers move away from the door, farther into the room, keeping plenty of space between myself and Chayce. There must be a strange look on my face as Adyr speaks.

"An unmated male around a yet-to-be-claimed female can cause issues," he clarifies, pointing to Chayce.

Right, the mate to his animal thing.

"It was part of the problem at the bar," Adyr continues, his eyes moving between me and Chayce as he seems hesitant to speak.

"Just ask," Chayce bites out.

"Regina, can you please give us your version of events from tonight?" Adyr asks gently, obviously not wanting to irritate his brother more than he already seems to be.

I explain how two of the guys basically started fighting over me, or at least who got my attention. Chayce starts to growl, I think? Without conscious thought, I reach back and take his hand, which he grips tightly, almost to the point of being painful.

Focusing back on Adyr and my explanation of events, I continue. "Two other guys stepped in, defending me and warning the first two away."

"If we take you to see them, all four, would you be able to tell us who started the fight and who was defending you?" Deakon chimes in, keeping wary eyes on Chayce. "It will make a difference when charges are filed."

Giving Chayce's hand a reassuring squeeze before responding, I prepare for an outburst before responding to Deakon.

"I would like to actually thank them for stepping in if that's possible." Squaring my shoulders, since I have gotten this far without Chayce objecting, I push on. "The situation spiraled out of control quickly. If it wasn't for their interference, who knows what would have happened..." My voice trails off as I let the accusation hang in the air.

Apparently, those were the wrong words. Before I can register what is happening, Chayce reaches over and lifts me out of the chair, setting me in his lap and wrapping his arms tightly around me. His body is vibrating as his chest heaves.

After several long and tense moments, Chayce grinds out, "Let's get this over with." Smoke drifts from his mouth and nose. It isn't the first time this has happened, but I disregard it for now, not feeling as if this is the appropriate time to ask about it.

Chayce stands abruptly, setting me on my feet. His brothers exit the office, giving us as much space as possible. Wrapping his arm around my shoulders and keeping me tucked into his side, Chayce guides me from the room. The tight grip he has on me makes walking awkward, but something tells me this isn't the time to mention his possessiveness.

We walk down a long hallway to the other side of the building, from where Chayce's office is located. The brothers are spaced out, leaning against the wall opposite the cell doors. Two of the men are in a cell together, while the other two each have separate cells. As we approach, all four men rise to their feet but remain along the far wall opposite the cell doors.

Oddly enough, my two saviors are paired together. Stepping forward, Chayce is reluctant to release me and only does so after I give him a glare over my shoulder.

"Gentlemen, I wanted to say thank you," I say sincerely as my hands begin to shake at the memory of earlier. "Getting into a fistfight was a little over the top, but you defended me. It is very much appreciated."

The two men bow their heads at me in appreciation and acknowledgment. Chayce steps forward as well, wrapping his arm around my shoulders before addressing the men.

"Thank you," he starts, "for protecting my mate." Chayce's voice is spoken softly, but in the silence of the jail, they are easily heard.

All four men whip their heads in his direction, reverently whispering the word "mate."

"The judge will be made aware of your actions," Chayce informs the two men before us. "While I'm unsure it will do any good, I will do what I can as appreciation for your actions," he finishes.

"That is the best we can ask for, Sheriff," one of the men says in response.

Chayce escorts me back to his office, leaving his brothers to deal with the next step. He sits in his chair and tries to pull me into his lap, but I push away from him, needing a little bit of space to get through my thoughts. Pacing his office and wringing my hands together, I start the conversation that I'm not sure I am ready for.

"All right, break this down for me," I say, trying to figure out where to start.

"Break what down?" Chayce asks, obviously confused about what I am referring to.

"You say that we are mates," I start, noticing him bristle, "fated to be together. What does that involve, exactly?"

"The mating is usually completed when we make love," he says, rubbing the back of his neck, his nerves showing.

There's something he isn't telling me, but I will circle back around on that in a minute.

"That's good to know, but it doesn't exactly answer my question," I say flatly.

"I thought I explained this," he says with a sigh. "Every paranormal has a fated mate. The one person meant and designed only for them," Chayce says, pausing to make sure that I am paying attention this time.

"So, what?" I state, pausing as my mind tries to fill in the blanks. "We have sex, which completes the bond, and then what?" I ask with a bit more attitude than is warranted.

"We spend the rest of our lives together," he says matter-of-factly.

"I have no say in this at all?" I question incredulously. "You have this…this…feeling or whatever," I stutter, waving my hand around Chayce's body. "And I am just supposed to go, 'Oh, okay then, let's fuck!'"

He cringes at both my phrasing and tone as my voice rises.

"Do you feel nothing for me?" Chayce asks in a defeated tone.

"I don't *know* you," I say in response. "How can I answer that honestly, having been in town for three, maybe four days? It isn't like we have spent more than ten minutes in each other's company. Tonight is the longest we have been in the same room. And yet, you expect me to just go along with this?"

Not giving Chayce any time to respond, I go back to his comment about bonding.

"What aren't you telling me?" I question, causing his brows to knit together.

"What do you mean?"

"You are hiding something," I accuse as a blush creeps into his cheeks. "You said that the mating is usually completed when we have sex. What is the rest of that?" I demand, fully facing him with my hands planted on my hips and staring him down.

"I have to bite you," he mumbles softly.

"Say what now?" I ask as my eyebrows hit my hairline.

Chayce moves to stand, but I hold my hand up in a stop motion, causing him to lower back into his chair.

"Depending on the paranormal." He pauses as if the delay will make his words sound any better. I roll my hand in a circular motion to get him to hurry up and get to the point. "Most paranormals, specifically shifters, leave a bite mark, sometimes called a mating mark. Vampires do it as well. Fae and witches are typically the exceptions," he explains, looking a bit sheepish.

"Let me make sure I understand this correctly," I state, pausing for dramatic effect. "We have sex, binding us together for life," pausing to take a breath before continuing, the color fades from Chayce's face, "during which you bite me."

"Yeah," is all he says in response.

"Is it safe to assume this bite will be visible? And leave a permanent scar on my body?"

"Yeah," he says again, causing me to grind my teeth together in annoyance.

"Being that you are sheriff here, I guess it is up to me to move here," I state, not exactly as a question. Chayce gets a hopeful look on his face.

"What are you?" I blurt out, catching him off guard.

"I am a dragon," he says flatly.

"Well, that explains all of the smoke," I say in return.

A brief knock interrupts our conversation as Brady opens the door to Chayce's office, not waiting for a response.

"Sorry," he says insincerely as his eyes dart between Chayce and me. "Chayce, we got another report of strange prints. They are fresh," Brady says. Chayce nods quickly, rising to his feet.

"Let's get you home," Chayce says, addressing me. "Duty calls. We can continue this conversation later," he adds, placing his hand on my lower back and guiding me out of the room.

As we step into the frigid outdoors, I wrap my arms around my body in an attempt to keep warm.

"Where is your coat?" Chayce grinds out as we reach his truck.

Jumping into the cab, I don't bother to answer. As I put my seatbelt on, Chayce jumps in, quickly closing the door behind him. He starts the truck and turns the heat up, but with the motor being cold, it's a waste of time.

It takes me a minute to try and figure out how his truck got here. The last I saw it, he left it in the middle of the street. The door behind me opens and Brady hops inside, earning a glare from Chayce.

"I figured I would save you a step," Brady says with a shrug. "Once you drop the little lady off, we can go straight to the pride," he says like his presence should be obvious.

Chayce doesn't comment; he just turns back around, throwing the truck into gear and heading to the rear of the Whiskey Genie.

Drying myself off after a long hot shower, I pull on some sweats and a long-sleeve T-shirt. Grabbing my phone, I play with it while brewing a cup of hot tea. Pressing the button before I think better of it, Rafferty picks up after two rings.

"Hey, G. What's going on?" His voice is full of concern, but also alert, letting me know I didn't wake him up.

"Do you have time to talk?" My voice wobbles, grabbing Raff's attention.

"Always, what happened?" he questions.

"What do you know about paranormals?" I ask him, repeating the question Chayce asked me just a short time ago.

"Quite a bit, actually," he says. When Raff speaks again, his voice is very serious. "Why?"

After launching into the story that Chayce gave me, Rafferty lets out a long whistle.

"Okay," he says with a sigh. "Here is what I can add. When a couple is mated, there is no screwing around. That's it, at least for the paranormal party. You are it for him. Now that he has found you, if you refuse to mate him, it can cause him issues."

I want to ask so many questions, but Rafferty keeps going.

"It's an all-or-nothing thing. If a paranormal never finds their mate, they just go on as they had been. Paranormals live longer lives than humans and once mated, if the mate is human, that person will gain longevity to their life as well. There is also a flip side, at least for some paranormals." Raff pauses as if warring with himself to finish. Just as I open my mouth for him to talk, he does. "Depending on the paranormal, if one mate dies, the other one follows shortly after."

His last sentence hangs in the air.

"Wow, okay," I say stupidly, not sure what else to comment with.

"Paranormals are also more rugged," I mouth the word "rugged" to myself as he keeps talking. "They have enhanced hearing, eyesight, and healing abilities. Oh," he says as a bit of an afterthought. "Whatever you do, do *not* ask someone what kind of paranormal they are. It is considered rude," he warns, causing me to cringe.

"Shit!"

Rafferty chuckles at my exclamation.

"If you are his mate, I don't think he is going to care. Just don't do it with anyone else," he warns. "Oh, and watch yourself around unmated males," Rafferty warns, not knowing I have already seen that display firsthand. "Did any of that help?" he asks, pulling my attention back to him.

"Yeah," I respond, resigning myself that I am now tied to the dragon sheriff and this tiny shifter town. "I guess I am going to be moving here," I admit out loud, causing my brother to chuckle.

"Do you want me to start packing for you?" Raff offers as if he has loads of spare time to take care of my stuff.

"I can hire a company to do it," I reply, not wanting to burden my brother with more projects. "There is too much for you to do, with work and everything," I offer as an out for him.

"Let me worry about it," he says firmly.

Rafferty and I talk a little longer before saying goodnight and hanging up.

Climbing into bed, I am exhausted but too tired to sleep. My mind is stuck on all things Chayce, from his job to his family and this sleepy little shifter town.

Without thought, my hands drift down my body, imagining they are Chayce's hands. One hand pushes my shirt up to my neck, exposing my bare breasts. Kneading the large globe and tugging on my hard nipple has my back arching off the bed.

The other hand sneaks under the waistband of my panties. My fingers easily slide between my folds, causing me to moan at the sensation. Sliding my fingers back and forth, gathering my juices, I rub my clit in soft circles. Teasing myself by increasing and decreasing the pressure, my arousal increases. Using my thumb to continue rubbing circles on my clit, my fingers glide into my channel. My orgasm is close. Pressing hard against my clit while pinching my nipple at the same time, I detonate, calling out Chayce's name as I peak. My fingers continue to move, working me through the last bit of my orgasm.

Lying here, catching my breath, I take a moment before getting up to wash my hands and clean up. Climbing back into bed, I drift off to dreams of dragons.

Dig's DINER
READERS WORLD

Chapter 21 - Chayce

My brothers are happy for me, to the point of being annoying. One thing became clear last night—whatever or whoever is leaving these prints around town, it isn't Regina. When the realization hit me, my shoulders sagged in relief.

The prints found on pride land were fresh. Considering Regina was either at the bar or with me, it couldn't have been her. This leaves us back to square one with no suspects.

It was late last night when I scheduled a meeting with all of the alphas for first thing in the morning. My dragon fought me all night, wanting to go and claim his mate now that we found her. He didn't care that I had work to do. I could tell Regina was apprehensive, and the uncertainty was killing me.

Trudging through the front door of my house last night, I looked around, trying to see it through Regina's eyes. It is still a surreal feeling that she is my mate. Shaking off my spiraling thoughts, I strip out of my clothes and climb into bed, praying that sleep takes me quickly.

The blaring of my alarm clock has me groaning. Climbing from my warm bed and stepping into the spray of the shower has me wide awake as the cold water hits me. It doesn't take me long to finish washing and then get dressed. Grabbing a coffee to take with me, knowing it's the first of many today, I head to the office.

Walking in, a smile crosses my lips when I spot Nora sitting at the reception desk.

"Good morning, Sheriff," she says with a pleasant smile.

"Good morning, Nora," I say, returning the greeting. "The alphas are coming in this morning for a meeting," I tell her since it isn't on my schedule. "Can you please show them to my office when they get here?"

"Sure thing, Sheriff," she says in reply as the phone rings.

"Thank you," I quickly say before she picks up the receiver.

Booting up my computer, it isn't long before all three of my brothers walk in. Crispin and Kyle are with them. As they get comfortable, I quickly email the triplets with the official employment proposal. Hitting send on the message just in time as Arek, Crispin, and Guri enter. Rising to my feet, I clap my hands together in order to get everyone's attention and start the meeting.

"Good morning, gentlemen. Thank you all for coming. I will do my best to keep this brief," I start, taking a deep breath as my speech continues. "We have had strange tracks on pack land, at both the den and the pride, not to mention the various break-ins at multiple businesses around town," I pause to check my notes before continuing, "This includes the Hamilton's grocery store. We have confirmed that the prints found are all the same, making it safe to assume this is the same individual." Rubbing my hand over the back of my neck, I hesitate to say the next words. "My primary suspect was cleared last night."

"Who was it?" They all ask at the same time, but not quite in unison. My brothers wear shit-eating-grins, already knowing the answer.

"That individual's name is irrelevant at the moment," I say sternly, hoping to move the conversation to a different topic. "As I said, she has been proven innocent."

It takes a moment before the men in my office catch my slip of the tongue. This time, they all, minus my brothers, *do* speak in unison.

"*She?*" they ask in shock and surprise.

Fuck. These guys are too damn smart. This is going to come back and bite me in the ass, I just know it.

"Wait a minute," Crispin, the cheeky bastard, says with a smirk on his face. "You wouldn't happen to be referring to the redhead that just *happens* to be your mate, are you?"

My only reaction to his question is the narrowing of my eyes. The rest of the men mull over Crispin's words before breaking into raucous laughter. My brothers even get in on the action, the traitorous assholes. Arek holds up his hand in a stop motion as I lean against my desk, arms crossed over my chest as I wait them out.

"Hold on…you…you mean to say…you thought that your mate, your one and only, was a thief and had been trespassing?" Arek manages to get out between bouts of laughter.

The entire room starts laughing even harder at my expense.

"Does she know?" Crispin asks as he wipes the tears of laughter from his eyes.

"Fuck no!" I bark out. "She barely believes me as it is. I assume she knows about paranormals, but who's to say she knows any. The last thing I want to do is scare her off." My volume raises with each word, my tone indignant.

My outrage at the simple question seems to set them off again. Pinching the bridge of my nose in frustration, I give them a few minutes to settle down.

"Are you done yet?" I ask in a droll tone.

Several more minutes go by before the laughter finally stops.

"All right," I say, a little louder than necessary, my annoyance obvious. "We need to figure out a plan to catch whoever, or whatever, this is running loose in the town."

Each of us tosses out different ideas on how to catch this person, ranging from setting traps, putting up trail cameras, or just ordinary surveillance. Catching them in the middle of committing a crime would be preferable but not likely.

"We need to get with the mayor and see about getting cameras installed around town," Guri says adamantly. "It is obvious that just having a town full of paranormal beings is not enough of a deterrent anymore. Not to mention, with the baseball season and pending casino opening, we might need them for something else."

His words make sense.

"Guri, do you have cameras in the store?" I question, hoping that if he does, we might get lucky and have the face of our thief.

"Well," Guri states, rubbing the back of his neck in frustration. "We do, but something happened. The cameras went offline for a twenty-minute period. After contacting the security company, they said the cause was on our end. We have nothing to help," he finishes with a defeated tone.

"That means whoever is doing this has the capability to disable cameras, possibly bypass security systems," Deakon says before I can.

Each of us groans in frustration, hitting another dead end.

The intercom on my desk buzzes, interrupting our meeting. Nora knows not to disturb us, as this is an important meeting.

"Excuse me, gentlemen," I say, slightly annoyed at the interruption. Picking up the receiver of my phone, I speak with Nora, my tone terse.

"Nora, we are in the middle of something."

"Sorry, Sheriff," she says nervously. "I have a Sergeant Chaney from the Boston Police Department on the line for you. He insisted on speaking with you now."

All eyes are focused on me. As I ignore them, Nora gets my full attention as my dragon starts to huff smoke from his nose.

"Put him through, Nora," I say a bit insistently.

"Sheriff Galloway here. How can I help you, Sergeant Chaney?" I purposely announce who I am speaking to and notice all three of my brothers' postures stiffen.

"Please," he says with a bit of humor. "We are pretty much family now, right?" he asks, catching me off guard. My dragon's pacing pauses and my chest heats for a different reason. If Regina mentioned our mating to her brother, does this mean she is accepting us? "Call me Rafferty," he says, focusing my attention back to him.

"Okay, Rafferty," I respond as every man in the room listens in, already aware of the fact this man is my mate's relation. "This can't be the reason you are calling me," I say shortly, concern starting to overwhelm me on the real reason.

"No," he says, blowing out a frustrated breath. "Has Gina told you about Jay yet?" he questions.

"Yes," I bite out at the mention of Regina's ex-boyfriend. Although, to a point I should thank him. If his treatment of her hadn't been so abhorrent, she wouldn't have made it here after fleeing Boston. "Can I put you on speakerphone?" I ask, as my thoughts spin to the possibility of Jay being our trespasser. "There are some gentlemen in my office that might need to hear what you have to say," I explain.

"Sure," he says in response. "Is it safe to assume they are also paranormal?" he questions, catching me off-guard.

Not answering his question right away, I hit the button on the phone so everyone can hear Rafferty, adding in any questions they might have.

"Is it safe to assume Regina discussed our situation with you?" I ask Rafferty instead of answering his question.

He chuckles in response before answering. "Yeah, you could say that. My partner is paranormal," he informs us, catching me off guard. "I was able to help fill in some gaps and am already starting to pack up Regina's apartment." My dragon sitting up straighter as my chest heats in anticipation of our mating. "You're welcome," Rafferty says flatly, causing the room to chuckle.

"Okay," I respond, drawing out the word, unsure of what else he wants me to say. "Why have you called?" I ask, trying to get back to the reason he called me. My tone is a little sharp at his blase attitude.

"Right," Rafferty says seriously before pausing. "We can't find Jaygon," he pauses again, letting that statement hang in the air. It takes a moment for his words to permeate my mating-induced brain fog. When it does, smoke billows from my nose at the implication. "My partner and I went to his apartment to talk to him. When we got there, the place was trashed. Our forensics lab was able to piece together some ripped-up documents and found several contracts Jaygon had signed."

"What does that have to do with Regina?" I ask, confused about what this asshole's business dealings have to do with my mate.

"Each of the contracts indicates Jaygon selling Regina to various men," he states angrily. "G told me that the last time she saw him, they were at some corporate dinner. Jay was trying to pimp her out. She got pissed and took a cab home. The next morning, she packed up and ended up with you," Rafferty explains.

Someone is threatening my mate, is the first thought that runs through my mind. The second is that this Jaygon guy thinks he has rights over her. Other men wanting to get their hands on her has both me and my dragon pissed. My hands partially shift as my dragon surges forward. As fingers turn into claws and scales transpose over the skin of my forearms, a growl seeps from my chest.

"All right, so we need to make sure Regina stays off their radar," one of my brothers says. "That shouldn't be too difficult, right?"

"Actually, no," Rafferty says. "We found tracking software on Jaygon's computer. From what we see, he installed something on Regina's phone and added a tracker on her car," he adds.

My eyes meet Kyle's, and he immediately pulls out his phone, presumably texting his father to start checking over her car since it's still at their garage. "Either way, Jay might be on his way there. Given your circumstances," Rafferty says, clearing his throat as he references my paranormal side. "I believe you have the ability to keep Regina safe and well-protected. This is a courtesy call to make you aware of what might be headed your way," he tacks on.

Every man rises to his feet, waiting for my orders—our trespasser problem put on hold, for now.

"Thank you, Rafferty," I say sincerely. "I appreciate you letting me know the situation. If you find anything else out, please let me know."

"Absolutely," he responds, as his voice turns soft. "She is more to me than just my sister," he adds, cementing my respect for him. "I am making sure he didn't plant anything in her belongings or in her apartment," Rafferty mentions after clearing the clogging emotion from his throat. "You might want to check her stuff. Make sure there aren't any extra trackers, especially her computer," he adds, causing my belly to clench at the thought.

"Got it," I say flatly, "thanks. Let's keep in touch."

Rafferty and I exchange cellphone numbers so we have direct contact with each other. Hanging up the phone, it takes me a moment to collect my thoughts. Turning to face the room, I address the alphas and my friends.

"Gentlemen, let's table our trespasser issue for the moment," I say, stating the obvious. "Kyle, please check over her car with a fine-tooth comb." He nods, shaking his phone back and forth.

"Dad is already starting the process," Kyle confirms, pocketing his phone.

"Thanks," I tell him. "If there is a tracking device, please bring it here," I request. "Oh, and if you can, try not to handle it too much. We might be able to get a fingerprint or two," I add as an afterthought.

Kyle nods before leaving the office, hopefully going to help his father check Regina's car.

"Crispin, can we get your wolves to expand their patrols to the entire city?" I question, thankful that at the moment, neither of our new businesses are open. He pulls his phone out, texting his pack, no doubt, or at least his betas.

"Can the three of you take to the air?" I ask, addressing my brothers. "Monitor the town and surrounding area."

The three of them immediately respond, Adyr leaving the room, unbuttoning his shirt as he goes.

Scrubbing my hands over my face, I speak to the men in front of me.

"Thank you for your patience and understanding," I state as an apology. "I understand that this is an unprecedented occurrence; hopefully, this is the last one, not the first one. If you will excuse me," I request, gathering my cell and keys off the desk. "Regina should hear this information from me, assuming Rafferty hasn't already called her. I also need to move Regina out of the apartment above the Whiskey Genie and into my house," I explain.

"My wolves are already out," Crispin interrupts. "If you could possibly release Madox and Tennyson? They can assist," he adds in the last part, playing on my concerns for Regina's safety.

"Yeah," I state absently. "They still need to face the judge," I tack on as a reminder.

Deakon moves to the door, keys to the cells in hand. Calling out to his retreating form, he waves his acknowledgment to my statement.

"Deakon, let them all out. We will figure out the charges later," I state, pushback from the mayor the least of my concerns at the moment.

Making my way to the door, I speak over my shoulder, not waiting around for a response.

"Call me if you find anything."

Thankful that the Whiskey Genie is close, it takes no time before I stand at Regina's door.

Chapter 22 - Regina

The pounding on the door matches the pounding in my head.

Sleep eluded me last night, and when I woke up this morning, my head felt like it would split in two. The cause would be understandable if I had gotten my drink on like I originally intended to. You know, before the whole bar fight and all.

Assuming it's Gypsy and the building is on fire due to the early hour, I don't bother to cover up. Yanking the door open and finding Chayce on the other side has me regretting that action.

He pushes his way inside, not waiting for an invitation, forcing me to step back. Chayce pulls the door closed behind him as I rub the sleep out of my eyes, trying to focus. Looking him over, the crazed look in his eye gets my attention.

"What is going on, Chayce?" I question, immediately on alert, having seen that look on Rafferty's face more times than I care to think about. "What's happened?"

Holding his hand out, indicating the couch, he places his hand at the small of my back, guiding me to it. I try and ignore the heat that spreads through my body at the innocent contact.

Taking a seat on the edge of the couch, Chayce looks around the room as if looking for a threat he hadn't noticed yet. Gripping his hand in mine to get his attention, he looks down at our connection before meeting my gaze.

"Rafferty called me," he says matter-of-factly.

Those three words have me jumping to my feet. My fingers twist the hem of my shirt as I pace.

"Why did he call you?" I ask accusingly.

Chayce falls to the couch, scrubbing his hands over his face before answering me, his head tipped back onto the top of the couch. After several long moments, he sits forward, placing his elbows on his knees.

"Jaygon is missing," he says flatly as his gaze moves to the floor, unable to maintain eye contact with me. "Rafferty and his partner had their forensics team restore papers that were found in his apartment." Chayce pauses as if regretting the news he has to give me. "Jaygon sold you to several different men in an attempt to cover a gambling debt. Rafferty suspects that he not only placed a tracker on your car but also your phone and possibly on your computer." His words are rushed as if he is trying to give me the news as quickly as possible.

"What?" I ask, my voice barely above a whisper.

My body starts shaking as anger takes hold. Chayce is instantly at my side, wrapping his strong arms around me. Pulling me tightly to his body, he rests his chin on the top of my head as tears of frustration begin to stream down my cheeks.

"We need to go through all of your stuff and make sure there is nothing else here," he informs me, as if delivering more bad news is going to send me over the edge. "Once we do that, we are going to move you to my house," he says, not giving me an option to object. "We will take care of your phone and computer in my office. If Jay tracked you here, it is too much of a risk for you to stay in this apartment alone," he explains, slightly softening his domineering orders.

Nodding my head rapidly, trying to figure out why Jay has done this—besides the obvious, my teeth start to chatter. Between the cold, since I am only wearing a T-shirt and underwear, and nerves, my body begins to shake uncontrollably. Chayce guides me to the bedroom so I can put some clothes on, not commenting on my state of dress or lack thereof.

Moving to the bathroom to collect myself and pack my toiletries, Chayce starts going through my luggage and personal items.

It took us almost two hours to go through my clothes, luggage, makeup, and personal belongings that I have with me. Thankfully, we didn't find anything. I still don't have the warm and fuzzies about it, feeling dirty, maybe even violated. Not to mention, I have watched one too many crime shows on television. I know they can hide that shit in a button or something.

When I mentioned this to Chayce, he gave me an incredulous look but said he understood and would do whatever I was comfortable with. Not wanting to leave a mess behind for Gypsy, we brought everything to the jail. Once we arrived, Chayce gave me a pair of sweatpants and a T-shirt so what I had on could be added to the rest. He secured both suitcases in their locker room. Chayce made a joke, trying and failing to lighten the mood, that if Jay did put a tracker in there that we missed, wouldn't he feel stupid tracking it to a sheriff's office?

His comment made me smile, but it was forced.

Deakon, Chayce's brother, is good with tech. The sheriff's office also has access to various programs the average person does not. It didn't take him long to confirm that Jaygon did, in fact, plant a tracking software on my phone. Thankfully, my computer is secure with a thumbprint scan, and he was unsuccessful in tampering with that.

Not wanting to take a chance, I call Emma from the desk phone, instead of my cellphone. She answers just before the call goes to voicemail.

"Hello?" she answers, sounding suspicious.

"Hey slut, it's me," I say, needing to hear a comforting voice.

"Bitch, what the fuck is going on?" she yells before continuing a barrage of questions, not letting me answer one before the next begins. "Why are you calling me from a sheriff's office? Do you need bail money? If you do, why didn't you call Rafferty first? Maybe he can use his police powers for good for a change instead of giving pretty girls speeding tickets all the time." The last part of her statement has a genuine smile stretching across my face.

Emma has a lead foot and thinks that just because I am related to a cop, she is exempt by proxy from getting citations. As soon as she takes a breath, I launch into the tale of what has happened over the past couple of days.

"Bitch, please tell me this is a bad joke?" she asks very seriously, offended on my behalf.

"I wish it was Em. Rafferty is going through all of my stuff and packing me up," I say seriously. "I told him to get a moving company to help, but he is insisting on doing it all himself."

"Back the fuck up a minute," she yells. "What do you mean Rafferty is packing your stuff?" Her question has an edge to it that isn't normal for my best friend.

"The sheriff, Chayce, is my mate, or I guess it is more that I am his mate," I explain. "Raff explained how it works. We just started discussing this last night, so the finer points of how this works is a little fuzzy," I finish.

Em sniffles. "You're leaving me," she says quietly.

Hearing the dejected tone come from my bubbly friend has my heart breaking, causing me to tear up. Hearing what Jaygon has done made me more angry and frustrated. Hearing my best friend go quiet and holding back tears has me shedding some of my own.

Chayce, who has been acting like he hasn't been listening to every word of our conversation, is suddenly at my side, wrapping an arm around me and holding me close.

"C...can I... What is he?" Emma stutters between sobs, not batting an eye at the fact I just told her that I am mated to a paranormal.

Knowing about paranormals for several years now is nothing new. They came out to mixed reviews, both for and against their kind. A handful of people that we know have come out loud and proud, but it never affected how we treated them or how they treated us. They are, after all, still people.

Looking up at Chayce, a resigned look is on his face. He gives me a subtle nod of acquiescence.

"He's a dragon." My words are just loud enough for her to hear me. As soon as Emma hears them, she starts screaming, forcing me to hold the phone away from my ear. Her sobs stop immediately, and her entire attitude changes.

"Does he have any brothers?" Emma questions very seriously.

Chayce releases me with a quick kiss on the forehead. Leaving the office, I notice his shoulders shaking in suppressed laughter. Once the door closes behind him, he loses control as loud laughter can be heard through the building.

"Actually, he does, three of them," I answer, once again holding the phone away from my ear in preparation for her to start yelling again.

"No shit!" Emma says excitedly. "I need to get myself some of that. Prepare for invasion. I am packing now."

Now it's my turn to laugh. Although knowing my friend, she isn't kidding.

"I will talk to Gypsy," I tell her. "You have a place to stay." Hoping that the bar owner won't mind. I don't want to assume that Chayce will be accepting of Emma staying in his house. Not knowing anything about his home, I don't even know how many bedrooms are in it. "Just make sure you check the weather report," I warn, thinking of my own stupidity. "This area can be dangerous. Oh, and look out for wolves on the road."

Something occurs to me that I urgently need to talk to Chayce about.

"I gotta go." My words are abrupt, cutting our conversation short. "Keep me updated on when you think you will be here," I state, not quite a question. "Miss you, slut!"

"You too, bitch. I will talk to you soon," she says before ending the call.

Hanging up the phone, I take a moment to collect myself. The past twenty-four hours have been a whirlwind. My life has turned upside-down in the blink of an eye, and I am struggling to keep up with all of the changes.

Moving to the door of Chayce's office, I pull it open, finding him talking to a man I haven't met yet. Their conversation halts as I make my way closer to them in the lobby area of the office. Chayce tilts his head, indicating his office, forcing me to change direction as the men head that way.

Once inside, Chayce approaches me, leaving the guy in the doorway.

"Regina Chaney. This is Jorden D'Angelo, Crispin's brother and beta. Jorden, this is my mate, Regina," Chayce says that last part proudly.

Jorden looks a lot like his brother, with shaggy blond hair, pale green eyes, and a soft smile.

"It's nice to meet you," I say, extending my hand to shake.

"It's nice to meet you too," Jorden says, warily watching Chayce from his position at the door. He makes no move to shake my hand, causing my brows to furrow.

"It's because we haven't completed the mating," Chayce whispers, letting me on to Jorden's movement, or lack thereof, is not to be taken offensively. "Did you need something?" he asks, distracting me from Jorden.

"Uhm, yeah," I say, forcing my attention away from the other man and toward Chayce. "A couple of things, actually. First, I need to talk to Gypsy." Chayce's brows knit together in confusion. "Emma is coming to town. She will need a place to stay," I explain, earning a nod of understanding in return. "Second, now that I know you all are paranormal, that wolf that I almost hit... Was that one of the townspeople?"

Jorden has a hand over his mouth, trying to hide a smile, but I catch it out of the corner of my eye despite his attempt. Cocking a hip and crossing my arms over my chest, I raise an eyebrow in his direction.

"Yeah, that is one of ours," Jorden informs me, telling me without directly saying that he and his brother, at least, are wolves. "He is also one of the ones that was arrested during the bar fight," he adds, making me feel guilty.

"Really?" I say in excitement, deciding that I have to do something nice for this guy since he pretty much saved me twice.

Jorden's gaze flicks to Chayce, suddenly nervous.

"Yeah, it was Madox," Jorden says with a cringe at Chayce's unasked question of who.

Chayce's body seems to grow as he stares Jorden down.

"Is Madox going to be a problem?" Chayce grinds out, smoke spilling from his nose and mouth.

Jorden starts shaking his head back and forth rapidly. Stepping closer to Chayce, I wrap my arm around his waist, and he deflates slightly. Soaking up the warmth of his body, I tune out their conversation.

Chayce kisses the top of my head before swinging me up into his arms. His body moves, bouncing me slightly. It's obvious we are now outside when the cold really hits me, causing me to burrow closer into Chayce's body. He settles me in his truck and closes the door once he has my seatbelt fastened. It doesn't take him long to climb in and start the vehicle.

"Where are we going?" I question, through a yawn.

"Our house," he says, his tone unreadable.

Butterflies fill my belly with his simple phrase. It amazes me that Chayce has already accepted, without a doubt, that I am his.

Dig's
DINER
READERS WORLD

Chapter 23 - Chayce

Having Regina in my home has my dragon calming down. For the first time in days, he is content. Deakon wasn't finished with Regina's phone when we were leaving the office, so we left it there. We had barely reached the town limits when she fell asleep.

After putting my sleeping mate to bed, I decide to take advantage of being home and work on some chores that have been neglected.

God bless my brothers. Trying to decide what to have for dinner, I realized there was nothing in my refrigerator. There wasn't even a jar of pasta sauce in my house, I called Brady with a list, and he ran to the store for me. It isn't much, as I don't know what Regina likes to eat, but it will get us through until we go shopping together.

A creak on the stairs lets me know Regina is awake. Stepping into the living room from my office, a small smile spreads across my face. Her hair is smashed on one side, and her face still has wrinkles from the pillow. It's the most adorable thing I have ever seen and I can't help the broad smile that stretches across my face.

"How was your nap?"

"Good," Regina says, covering her yawn with her hand. "Do you have any coffee?"

Gripping her shoulders, I steer her toward the kitchen. Helping her into a chair, my hands get busy making her a cup of coffee. It's something I drink a lot of, not knowing what will happen, especially during the winter months. I could be awake for days at a time dealing with the snow and whatever else pops up around town.

A smile tips my lips once she is settled, cradling the warm cup in her hands. Thoughts of spending our lives like this warm my chest. Sitting down next to her, I push a strand of hair behind her ear. Regina leans into my touch.

Smoke escapes my nose, causing her eyes to widen.

"You have been doing that a lot," Regina states, taking a sip of her coffee. "Is that normal?"

"Sorry," I say as heat floods my cheeks in embarrassment. "He is happy. There are times when he does what he wants to do, taking me along for the ride."

A slight blush appears on her cheeks, and she twists the coffee cup in her hands. As I open my mouth to ask what is on her mind, Regina beats me to it.

"Can...can you show him to me?" she asks timidly.

My grin widens in excitement. "Absolutely!"

Regina relaxes slightly at my enthusiasm.

"What are you thinking?" I question.

She slumps back in her chair, keeping a tight grip on the cup and holding it to her chest, refusing to make eye contact.

"A lot has happened in a very short period of time," she says flatly.

"Is there anything you want to talk through?" I ask nervously. "I want you to be happy here."

"Honestly, there hasn't been enough time for it all to sink in," she says, biting her bottom.

"Okay, let's go through a few things, and I can answer any questions you might have as we go. How does that sound?"

Regina nods in agreement, which I take as a good sign. "Rafferty is packing up your belongings, right?" I ask rhetorically, continuing after Regina gives a slight nod. "Once they arrive, we can sort through everything, and if there is stuff here that you want to change, we can. If you want to buy all new stuff, that is an option as well." If Regina wants to set the place on fire and start over, I am happy to do that. Whatever is going to make this woman happy.

She releases a breath, resting her head on my shoulder. My dragon lies down with an expression that can only be contentment, as this is the first time Regina has initiated contact.

"Are you hungry?" I ask, wanting to make sure my mate wants for nothing.

"Not really," she says in a resigned tone.

"What do you want to do?" I ask, having no idea what she needs right now. Regina might get tired of my twenty questions, but eventually, something is going to spark her interest.

"Honestly," she says, pausing to take a deep breath. "I don't know. Maybe just sit and watch some television?"

Helping Regina to her feet, I escort her into the living room and sit down. Maneuvering our bodies, Regina sits in the vee of my legs as one runs along the length of the couch and the other is on the floor. She uses my chest as a backrest as I wrap my arms around her waist.

Reaching for the remote, the television powers on, and I bring up the menu before handing it to Regina. Hopefully, she finds something to watch as nothing more than a distraction.

Chapter 24 - Regina

Just vegging out on the couch for a while and sipping my coffee has done a lot for my state of mind.

Chayce reluctantly got up and made us some dinner, neither of us really wanting to move. Once we ate and cleaned up the dirty dishes, we made our way back to the couch. This is where we are now. Both of us are lying on our side, facing the television. With him behind me and his arm draped over my waist, Chayce draws random patterns on my skin. The innocent touch is soothing.

There is something about this man that settles me.

Deciding to be brave, I push my ass back into him, wiggling a little. His hand stills immediately as his chest heats. Neither of us says anything as I repeat the motion. This time, his chest rumbles.

Chayce moves his hand to my hip, playing with the hem of my shirt. Slowly, he moves it up, exposing skin above the waistband of my pants. The random patterns resume over the newly exposed flesh.

Pushing my shit higher with each pass, Chayce moves his hands, massaging the muscles of my lower back. It feels so good a moan slips out, causing him to still his movements. Looking over my shoulder at him, my tone is one of annoyance.

“Why did you stop?”

“You moaned…” he says, stating the obvious.

“Yeah, and? It feels, or felt, good,” I say with a *duh* style tone. "until you stopped."

Instead of replying, Chayce pushes his hips forward. His hard cock presses into my back. My eyes bug out at the size of that thing, worried if it will fit. Deciding to take control of the situation, I roll over to face him, almost falling off the couch in the process.

Leaning up, pressing my lips to his, it isn't long before he takes control of the kiss. Nibbling on my lower lip, he takes it between his teeth, biting gently. Tossing a leg over his hips, our centers line up almost perfectly. As our tongues duel, our hips start to grind against each other, and our breathing becomes heavy.

Chayce's hand moves up under my shirt. When he reaches my breast, he kneads it, letting out a soft moan of appreciation. Yanking the cup of my bra down, he frees my tit and plays with my nipple. Releasing my lip, Chayce trails kisses along my jawline and neck.

The shrill sound of his cell phone ringing is like a bucket of ice water has been dropped on us. Chayce lowers his head to the crook of my neck, mumbling expletives under his breath. The ringing stops and starts right back up again. Helping me sit up, he pulls the annoying device from his back pocket.

"What?" he barks into the phone, causing me to chuckle. I bury my head in his chest in an attempt to muffle the sound.

He heaves out a heavy sigh as he urges me to my feet. Fixing my bra, knowing that our night has been interrupted, I move to the far end of the couch. Chayce stands, heading to the kitchen with the phone still at his ear. Pocketing his keys, keeping the phone wedged between his neck and shoulder, his free hand moves to his crotch, where he adjusts himself.

"Fine," he sighs out. "See you in ten." He ends the call and pockets his phone.

A soft smile graces my lips at his dejected look.

"Duty calls, I presume?"

Walking toward me, Chayce gives me a quick nod in answer to my question. Rising to my feet, meeting him halfway across the room, my arms automatically go around his neck as he leans down to kiss me. Just as the kiss turns heated, he pulls back. Placing his forehead against mine, "I apologize for this."

"It is your job—don't worry about it," I scoff as if I have the right to get offended.

"When I get back, can we pick up where we left off?" he asks hopefully.

"I will be naked and waiting," I quip. My words hit their mark, causing him to shiver.

"Thanks," he grinds out. "My dick was already hard. Now I could pound nails into a two-by-four with the damn thing."

Suppressing a chuckle at his state of arousal, I urge him toward the door.

"Go save the town," I say in a strict tone. "Just be safe," I add on.

"Okay, make yourself at home. It is, after all, your house now too," he reminds me.

Placing a chaste kiss on my lips, Chayce walks out the door through the kitchen.

It occurs to me that this is my life now. Worrying about Rafferty has always been a burden of having a loved one on the police force. Now, being mated or married or whatever, I will constantly be on edge, worrying about Chayce coming home.

Padston is not Boston by a long shot. Most of the town is paranormal, and being a dragon, Chayce is *the* top predator. How easy is it to hurt or maim a dragon?

Ugh! Just as I start to wind down, more questions run like a marathon in my head. I need something stronger to drink than just coffee.

Dig's
DINER
READERS WORLD
BOOKS

Chapter 25 - Chayce

Arriving at the station, Crispin, Kyle, Arek, Guri, and all three of my brothers greet me. Not bothering to say a word, I continue to move to my office. I assume they are all following me, at the moment, I don't really care either way.

Throwing myself into the chair behind my desk, I cross my arms over my chest, glaring at each man as they enter the room. All of them give me strange looks due to my behavior.

"What is your problem?" Crispin asks, an eyebrow raised in question.

"Cockblocking asshole, what do you want?" I grind out. They are all old enough—they can fill in the blanks of what I am *not* telling them.

It doesn't take them long to do so either, as almost immediately, every one of these assholes starts laughing uproariously.

"You're pouting?" Arek asks.

Glaring at him, speaking through gritted teeth, I grind out. "When you meet your mate and start getting down to business for the first time and get interrupted, let me know how it feels."

The laughter stops abruptly.

"All right, what happened?" I snap. Regina was right—no matter how bad my dick hurts, my job comes first.

"We have more tracks. One of the other stores in town is missing general home items, blankets, flashlights, lanterns, that sort of stuff," Brady states.

"We have merchandise missing as well," Guri adds.

Leaning forward, I lay my arms on the desk and fold my hands together, my mind spinning.

"All right, so whoever this is coming into and around town, taking items for them to survive on," I say.

"Are there any caves or some type of natural shelter in the area?" I question, my eyes moving from man to man. "They have to be somewhat close, but where did they come from?" My flurry of questions has each man looking pensive, contemplating the area of land around their homes.

"What about the game lands? That is a lot of ground to cover," Kyle mentions.

"Deakon, do your computer thing," I say. "Start charting around town; we will take small sections at a time, as many of us from each clan as possible," I continue as my mind spins at the possibilities. "We will start around town, working our way out. If we find where they are hiding, we can always wait for them if they aren't there."

"Are you talking about a system rescue teams often use where they space themselves out, all moving in a line?" Kyle asks.

"Yes, to a degree," I answer, rubbing my chin. "Instead of hit or miss searches, we will throw all of our resources into a concentrated area and move on. Every other person will be shifted since senses are better in shifted form, and we will use a radial pattern, using this office as the center point," I explain.

"That might work," Crispin says in agreement. "Then again, if our trespasser is watching us, they might move."

"That is a chance we might need to take. Hopefully, we will get lucky. If we do chase them out of their current hiding space, we can find a fresher scent to track them better," I argue. "Let's meet here at eight tomorrow morning and get started."

After agreeing, our small crowd breaks up, each of the other alphas going their own way. My brothers lag behind and as soon as the office is empty, they turn to me.

"Regina's phone is finished if you want to take it with you. She left her computer here as well," Deakon says. "How large do you want the areas set up for the search?"

Scrubbing my hands over my face, my words are muffled. Moving them, I start over with my answer. "We will have at least twenty people. Set it up like pie slices, figuring there are three-ish, maybe, feet between each person? Go from there," I tell him. “We can adjust if we have more or less if you want to add that in your calculation somehow.”

“Okay, I will work on that now so we are ready for tomorrow morning,” Deakon says before leaving my office.

“It should be a quiet night tonight. We only need one of you on duty. Whoever is going to sleep can run and any calls we get tomorrow while everyone else searches for our trespasser,” I say to Brady and Adyr, letting them choose who works.

“I’ll stay, Brady can go home,” Adyr says.

Jumping to my feet, I address the pair. “All right, I am heading back home. Unless the town is on fire, don’t call me,” I state emphatically, causing the two morons to laugh as I head to my truck.

Once home, I am disappointed to find Regina fast asleep in my bed. Letting out a soft groan of frustration, I strip down to my boxers and climb into bed behind her. Pulling her sleeping form into my body, my arm bands tightly around her waist.

It takes a minute for me to realize she wasn’t teasing me before I left—she is naked.

Chapter 26 - Regina

Hot. I am so hot.

Trying to move is next to impossible. It takes my sleep-filled brain a minute or two to realize where I am and what the source of the heat is.

Chayce has me pinned against his body.

Naked and waiting is how he found me, okay, asleep too, since I got tired of waiting up, not knowing how long he would be gone. A quick glance at the clock lets me know how early it is, and I groan into the pillow to muffle the sound. Going back to sleep would be the right thing to do. However, the coitus interruptus earlier has me a bit on edge.

Managing to wiggle enough to roll over, my hands now have access to Chayce's naked chest. Damn, this man is chiseled. His breathing remains even, but his chest gets hotter, letting me know his dragon is awake. My fingertips lightly brush over every ridge of muscle in his chest and abdomen. Slowly, my hand moves south toward the large python in his boxers. My breath hitches at the size as my hand rubs over the outside of his underwear.

"If you keep that up, it's going to get mad and spit at you," a deep voice says, startling the shit out of me. I would jump but being wrapped up in Chayce's hold it's impossible.

Looking up at his face, the smirk he wears has me feeling bold.

My fingers grip the waistband of his boxers, and I slowly wiggle them off his hips and down his legs, freeing his large, hard cock. He kicks off the offending garment as I reach out, gripping his dick and giving it a squeeze before moving my hand up and down. Chayce lets out a soft groan as he throws his head back. Moving toward the foot of the bed, I bend slightly, taking his length in my mouth. Chayce hisses at the feeling. Slowly bobbing my head up and down his shaft, my hand grips the bottom, moving in tandem with my mouth.

Hollowing out my cheeks, sucking hard, he starts to thrust his hips, unable to remain still. Chayce catches himself, grabbing a fist full of my hair and guiding my speed and movements. My free hand moves to fondle his balls as I give his cock a tight squeeze.

"Fuck yes," he hisses out, "just like that. Fuck, fuck, fuck!"

Doubling my efforts and taking as much of his length down my throat as possible, it doesn't take long before Chayce is coming, and coming, and coming. I swallow as much of him down as I can, but there is so much; some of it runs down my chin, dripping on his crotch.

Releasing my hair, his hand falls to the bed as Chayce catches his breath. Standing up, I walk into the bathroom to brush my teeth; once finished, I grab a warm washcloth to help him clean up.

Cleaning up the remnants of his release, Chayce starts to get hard again under my hand. Saying nothing but giving him a questioning look, complete with a raised eyebrow, he shrugs unapologetically.

After tossing the washcloth into the bathroom, I climb back into bed, my back to his front. Chayce starts kissing the length of my neck, causing me to shiver.

"That was fantastic," he says in a whisper. "Will you let me take care of you now?" he asks as his hands travel up and down the side of my body.

Patting the hand resting against my belly, "Tomorrow," I tell him, my yawn cutting off his argument. The heat emanating from his chest, accompanied by the rumble of his dragon, has me falling right back to sleep.

Unsure what woke me, as my eyes open, they widen in shock at finding Chayce between my legs, his face hovering above my pussy.

"My turn," is all he says in warning before feasting on my flesh.

Chayce swirls his tongue in a circle over my clit, causing my back to bow. Intermittently he bites and sucks as he slides his fingers through my wetness. As he continues to lick, bite, and suck, two fingers slide inside my channel, rubbing my outer wall.

"Yes," I say with a moan, dragging out the word.

Chayce hums and the vibration only adds to the sensation. Gripping his head, it's my turn to control his movement, guiding him where I need him in order to fall over the edge of bliss. He follows my lead, and it isn't long before his name gets called out as my orgasm peaks.

"Chayce!"

Lapping up my orgasm, his fingers continue to move in and out of my body. Slowly, he starts kissing his way up my torso. When he reaches my breasts, he alternates between my nipples, sucking on each one in turn. His eyes are glued to mine, and I can only guess he is trying to gauge my mood. Unsure what Chayce sees within them, he comes to a decision.

Lining himself up with my channel, he enters me slowly, giving me every opportunity to have him stop. Inch by glorious inch of flesh-covered steel is pushed inside my body. The stretch feels good and a bit painful at the same time. Gripping the sides of his head, I pull him forward, capturing his lips and tasting myself on them. I convey, without words, how much I want this. We both let out a moan as Chayce fully seats himself.

I don't remember ever feeling this full. It's almost to the point of being painful. Lifting my hips, trying to urge him to move, Chayce gets the point as his hips start to piston.

Releasing my lips, he lowers his head to suck on my nipples. My hands move to hold them up for him as he lets out a groan of appreciation. His pace picks up, hips snapping hard with each thrust forward. We are both moaning and grunting in pleasure. Chayce abandons my tits, causing me to suppress a groan of frustration.

Sitting back on his heels, Chayce lifts my legs, urging me to sit up to straddle him. The new angle is more intense than the previous one, hitting my cervix with each thrust. Wrapping my arms around his neck, our chests rub together. The rough texture of his chest hair rubbing against my nipples is a new sensation. One I definitely like. Our bodies move in tandem as Chayce kisses me hard. Breaking the kiss, he licks, bites, and kisses his way across my jaw and down my neck. I am so lost in sensation that what he does next catches me off-guard.

At the juncture of my neck and shoulder, Chayce licks, causing me to shiver slightly at the odd sensation. In the next moment, his teeth are sinking into my flesh, triggering my orgasm. He continues to suck on my neck, teeth firmly planted, as his hips stutter, finding his own release.

After a few more hard thrusts, his movement slows as he unclenches his jaw, licking up the blood that escapes the fresh wound. Chayce warned me about the bite. It isn't what I expected it to be. Yes, at first, there was pain, but when it morphed into pleasure...wow. Without breaking our connection, he lowers us back to the bed, placing a soft kiss on my forehead as he wraps his arms around my body.

It takes several minutes for both of us to catch our breath, our heavy breathing is the only sound in the room. As my breathing slows, the pull of sleep drags me down, more content than I have ever felt.

Dig's
DINER
READERS WORLD
CARDS
BOOKS

Chapter 27 - Chayce

Regina is officially mine. My dragon is preening. He has his mate.

Lying here, with Regina in my arms and my cock still inside her, my world is whole. My dick is already starting to get hard again. Knowing that I will need to take her again soon to avoid my dragon breaking loose, my eyes close, thankful for the amazing gift in my arms.

Regina's steady breathing lets me know that she has fallen asleep. With her tight sheath wrapped around me, I can't help myself as my hips start to move of their own accord. She lets out a soft moan of pleasure, unconsciously pushing her ass backward into my pelvis.

My hands roam over her body as she starts to wake from the barest of slumbers. I would say that I feel guilty keeping her from resting, but I truly don't. Grasping her breast, a moan escapes me. I knew that once I had my hands on her tits, it would be game over. Thoughts of fucking them and giving her a pearl necklace have my hips stuttering.

Spinning Regina to face me, I bend down to kiss her, my tongue fucking her mouth in the same rhythm I fuck her pussy. Moving my hips faster, my hand drifts down to rub her clit. Her pussy grips me even tighter, which I didn't think that was possible. With both of us on our sides, I pull one of her legs over my hip and start to move faster, chasing my release.

Regina surprises the shit out of me when she leans forward, biting my neck in the same place on my body as I bit hers. While her teeth don't sink into my flesh the same way mine sunk into hers, the effect is still the same. Both of us yell out as we climax together. My thrusts slow as cum continues to fill her channel.

We stay in that position until our breathing returns to normal. After several moments, Regina starts to pull away. My dragon grumbles at the separation, causing Regina to chuckle.

"Shower," she says, her words stilted. "Not sure my legs are going to support me, but I am a sticky mess."

Pulling from her body, Regina winces slightly. Leaving her in bed, I enter the bathroom and start filling the bathtub. With the tub filling, I go back into the bedroom and find Regina lying with her arm over her eyes. A soft chuckle escapes me as I bend to pick her up. Heading back into the bathroom, I gently set Regina on her feet. Once she is steady, she climbs into the warm bath. Glancing over her shoulder at me, a smirk on her face, she winks as a soft moan escapes her. Moving forward, Regina makes space for me to climb in behind her.

Once we are settled, we take advantage of our position. Washing each other's bodies, our hands explore every part of each other, some touches lingering longer than others.

"How sore are you?" I question as my cock gets hard again.

Regina's head falls back against my chest as she peers up at me.

"Sore enough that you are going to have to wait a few hours before fucking me again," she says with a laugh.

Smiling softly at her, I lean down, kissing my mark on her neck. She shivers slightly before leaning back against my chest. We stay like that until the water gets cold.

Sitting at the kitchen table, as I prepare for the day, Regina sips her coffee as I make us some breakfast.

"Thank you for bringing my computer back," she says, twisting the chord in a nervous gesture. "What happened last night, that you ran out of here so fast, or can't you tell me?" She lifts her head to make eye contact.

I hesitate and rub the back of my neck. She needs to know my initial thoughts regarding the timing of her in town and the thefts that have been happening. If one of the others brings it up in front of her without me explaining, there is no telling how mad Regina is going to be. Steeling my spine, deciding to rip the bandage off, my tone is soft.

"There is something you need to know," I start, pausing to collect my thoughts on how best to explain this. I really enjoy fucking her and hope to do so again later. "It isn't bad, per se." She raises an eyebrow at my hesitation. "I just want you to hear this from me and not one of the others," I state cryptically, still not sure how she is going to take this.

Regina has an expectant look on her face as if my hesitation is tedious.

"We, the town that is, have had a lot of unknown prints showing up around town," I start explaining, keeping a close eye on her facial expression to gauge how she is feeling. "It was first on pack lands, then the den, and then the pride. It all started right before you got into town." She raises an eyebrow at me, no doubt jumping to conclusions. The rest of my explanation comes out rapidly, wanting to get through this as quickly as possible. I make a mental note to try and stop at the flower store today, to help smooth things over. "The timing was terribly suspicious as the exact night you were in town, the Hamilton's store was robbed." Now, both of her eyebrows are in her hairline.

Rubbing the back of my neck, hesitating on this next part, knowing Regina is going to be pissed. Looking back at it now, she has every right to be.

"Deakon ran a full criminal background check on you at my request," I say, cringing slightly in preparation for her outburst.

Keeping a close eye on her, Regina sits there, staring at me. Neither of us move or say anything, barely breathing. Opening my mouth to speak, she does something unexpected—she laughs.

My eyes are wide, unsure what to do or how to respond. Regina has tears streaming down her face as she continues to laugh, wrapping her arms around her middle. The full-on belly laugh catches me off guard.

"Y-you th-thought I-I was st-stalking yo-your town?" she stutters out between laughs.

Now I feel really stupid. Regina starts coughing, trying to catch her breath. Taking a step in her direction, she holds a hand up, halting my movements.

I stand there, mid-step, waiting for her to calm down. After several minutes, she wipes the tears off her cheeks, facing me, anger now blazing in her eyes. Regina sits back in her chair, arms crossed over her chest. This is the reaction I was prepared for, although after her laughter, it takes me a few minutes to catch up to the emotional rollercoaster. I feel like I have whiplash.

"Tell me..." Regina starts. "How did you determine that it wasn't me? Or do you still think it's me?" Her voice has an edge to it, letting me know my answer better be one to her liking.

"There was an incident," I say softly. "You were with me when it happened. There was another one last night, and you were here," I say, letting my voice trail off.

"So, assuming that I can't be in two places at once, you deemed me not guilty by process of elimination," she bites out, causing me to cringe.

"Since we haven't caught the guilty party, yes," I say guiltily.

"Thanks," she says, just barely above a whisper.

While I haven't known her long, any man with a brain knows that this isn't good. My mind spins, scrambling on what to say or do to make this right. My phone rings, breaking through the silence and tension in the room. Swiping my finger across the screen without looking to see who it is, Deakon's voice has my head snapping toward the clock.

"Where are you?" Deakon bites out. "Half the town is here, waiting for you."

"Shit! On my way."

Ending the call, my phone gets stuffed back into my pocket as I scramble to plate the food I made. Shutting everything off, I grab my keys and step toward Regina. She holds her hand up to stop me again. I am beginning to hate that move.

"You know that you are in the doghouse, right?" she asks.

"Yeah," I acknowledge, making sure that she knows, that I know, how angry she is.

"Be safe," is all she says before grabbing her laptop and heading into the living room.

Being dismissed, I go to work. Maybe if we get lucky, someone will give me a hard time, giving me an outlet for my frustration.

Chapter 28 - Regina

Chayce's dejected look made my chest hurt. He made me mad, though, and that shit is not excusable. It's only been a short while since I skidded into town, literally, and there has to be some type of learning curve. The fact that he told a bunch of other people his suspicions pisses me off.

Not that I have my phone and that it's safe to use—it's time to make some calls.

"Hello," the tired voice says from the other end.

"Why didn't you tell me about the contracts and that Jaygon is missing?" I yell, not bothering with pleasantries with Rafferty.

"What the fuck time is it?" he grinds out, his voice still groggy from sleep.

"Eight a.m."

"Fuck," he says. Shuffling in the background reaches me. "Hold on a minute, I gotta piss," Rafferty says just before the line goes silent.

My nose crinkles at his crass words. That was more than he needed to share, but at least he didn't take the phone in with him. There are certain things a sister doesn't need to hear, bodily function or not.

"All right," he heaves out. "While I make some coffee, what is your problem?" Rafferty questions, ignoring my opening statement.

"When we talked, why didn't you tell me?" I question, fighting back tears of frustration. "Why didn't you tell me that Jaygon was missing? Or about the contracts? Instead, you called Chayce?" I spew rapid-fire questions at my idiot brother, not giving him a chance to answer one before throwing the next one at him. My voice gets louder with each question.

"Do we need to do this now?" Rafferty gripes.

"Yes," I state emphatically. "He pissed me off. You have pissed me off. Chayce is busy, so you are getting my attention right now."

"How the fuck does that work?" Raff bites out, tossing my anger right back at me. "Your boyfriend fucks up, and somehow it's my fault?" His voice gets higher as he speaks.

"You also fucked up," I respond as a reminder. "You still haven't answered my question. Why. Didn't. You. Tell. Me?" I bite out each word since I have asked three times now.

Rafferty mutters a soft "fuck" as the coffee machine gurgles in the background.

"He can protect you," Rafferty finally answers, referring to Chayce. "What kind of shifter is he anyway?" He changes the subject.

"Dragon," I say, sighing loudly as I try to get him back on track. "Why are you being cagey about this?" My disappointment in being left out is obvious.

"G, he needed to know what was going on," Rafferty starts to explain. "He has access to more information in the criminal database. I am too far away to protect you. Not only that, he is the town sheriff. Chayce needs to be on alert due to the potential crime element possibly heading in your direction," he finishes, causing me to pout at the reasonable explanation.

Rafferty's level-headed explanation takes some of the wind from my sails. Deciding it's my turn to change the subject, I smirk, not that he can see it.

"Emma is coming to see me."

He huffs out a chuckle at that.

"That place won't know what hit them with the two of you together," Rafferty says with a smile in his voice. "What made that happen?"

"She had a meltdown when I told her that I was moving here," I explain. "Once she heard about Chayce, she did a one-eighty, asking if he has brothers." Rafferty starts laughing at this, knowing how Emma is. "As soon as she found out that he did, she started packing. There are more men in this town than women, and they are all paranormal," I continue, causing Rafferty to whistle in surprise. "I have actually met most, if not all, of the alphas. They seem nice," I tell him, hopeful that my best friend will finally find some happiness.

"Of course, they are going to be nice to you," he says as if I am stupid. "Chayce could eat them if he wanted to." Rafferty laughs, causing my brows to furrow.

"Would you be okay if Em stops to see you before she leaves town?" I ask, trying to ignore the images of Chayce's dragon on a rampage, eating the other alphas. "I really could use some more warm clothes. Not to mention that I am ready to ditch everything I have for fear that Jay bugged my stuff." I shudder.

"Shit," he exclaims. "Yeah, I can make that happen. I am off today, so I will go back to your place and start checking everything and pack a bunch of stuff," he says, automatically switching into protector mode. "Make sure she has my number and have her call me when she is ready to go. Since I am up," he says, emphasizing the *up* since it's obviously my fault for waking him. "I will grab a quick shower and some food, then head out."

"Thank you," I say sincerely, "love you."

"Love you too, G," he responds. "We got this."

Forcing back tears, it takes a moment for the knot to clear from my throat before calling Em.

"Hey, bitch," she answers, chipper as usual. "What is going on?"

"Assuming you were serious last night about coming down here." I pause in case she has changed her mind.

"Shit yeah, I am serious as a heart attack," she quips.

"Could you please stop by my place so Rafferty can give you some of my stuff?" I ask before quickly tacking on, "You wouldn't mind bringing it with you, right?"

"Abso-fuckin-loutely!" she cheers, making me laugh. "Tell me about these brothers," she demands, changing the subject.

"Let me tell you, there is more man meat in this town than a girl would know what to do with," I tell her, chuckling as she gasps audibly.

"What do you mean?" she questions.

"The little bit I have seen, there are very few women. The alphas are all hot as hell. Oh, I met one of the betas too. If you can't or don't find a man of your own in this town, girl, something is wrong," I tease.

"We will see," Emma says skeptically. "Goodness knows my love life or lack thereof, can use a good kick in the ass."

"How long before you think you will be here?" I ask, making a mental note to talk to Gypsy about her staying above the bar.

"My plans are to be there by the end of next week. There are some things that need to be cleared up first," she says, a hint of sadness in her voice.

"Is something wrong?" I asked, concerned for my normally exuberant bestie.

"Nah, I'm good," she says, brushing off my concern.

"Okay," I respond, not convinced that she isn't hiding something. "As you can tell, my phone is good to go. Deakon did some computer thing and removed the tracker," I say, stating the obvious but changing the subject.

"Ohh, what is Deakon?" Em says, her enthusiasm front and center again.

"He is one of Chayce's brothers," I respond with a giggle of my own, explaining who, not what Deakon is.

"Nice!" Em responds with a yell. "All right, if I ever plan on getting on the road, I need to get my ass moving,"

"Keep me updated on your plans and where you are at," I instruct. "By the way, when you get into the mountains, be careful. My GPS wasn't working right—the signal sucks."

"Will do. I will also call Rafferty and grab some of your stuff," she reassures me before ending the call.

Grabbing a fresh cup of coffee, after we say our goodbyes, I grab my computer and head to the couch, planning on getting some work caught up.

Dig's
DINER
READERS WORLD
BOOKS

Chapter 29 - Chayce

We have been moving through and around town all day. It has been a very cold, blustery day, making me thankful for the internal heat my dragon creates. As promised, all of the alphas are here, and each brought several of their people. With the amount of manpower we have, I am optimistic we will find something soon. The last thing we need is a rogue shifter or whatever they are. This scenario has the potential to become a proverbial keg of dynamite as the town residents defer to their animal side in order to preserve our way of life.

"Chayce, it's almost dark," Crispin says, drawing me out of my spiraling thoughts. "What do you want to do?"

Checking my watch, I decide to call it a night. Letting out a sharp whistle to get everyone's attention, Crispin and I wave them in.

"Thank you, all of you, for coming out today and helping," I say, keeping my voice louder than usual so that the large crowd can hear me. "We are calling it quits for today. Let's meet here at seven tomorrow morning. That should give us an extra hour of daylight to work with." The group starts to disperse with mutters of "good night" and "see you in the morning," while others give an absent-minded wave of acknowledgment.

A few groans reach my ears, and I suppress a smirk about the early hours. In the end, this should all pay off and help us find our thief and trespasser.

Driving a little faster than normal, my dragon is pushing me to get home to our mate. A grin takes over my face at the thought. It falls just as quickly as memories of Regina's irritated glare just before I walked out the door this morning. Slamming my hand on the steering wheel, I realize I forgot to grab flowers and curse myself.

Barely having the truck in park and shut off before I hop out, my footsteps are rapid. Just before reaching the door, the smell of oregano and garlic reaches my nose, causing my stomach to rumble in appreciation. Stepping into the kitchen I spot Regina at the stove. Turning around with a plate in hand, she smiles at me.

"I had to improvise on dinner; hopefully, you like it," she says, biting her lip.

"If it tastes as good as it smells, that won't be an issue," I tell her honestly.

She takes the plate over to the table and sets it down. Following behind her, as soon as she turns around, I pull her into my arms, burying my nose in her hair.

"Hi," she says softly. "Was your day okay?"

Instead of speaking, I lean down, capturing her lips with mine. Reluctantly breaking the kiss and stepping back slightly, she tries to break from my hold.

"The garlic toast is going to burn if I don't get it," she says, placing her hands on my chest, trying in vain to push me away. "Have a seat." Regina moves back to the stove.

Doing as told, I pull out a chair and sit down, my mouth beginning to water. Memories run through my head as I try to remember the last time someone else cooked a meal for me, other than going to the restaurant or grabbing takeout. The sound of a chair scraping across the floor brings me back to the present.

Grabbing a slice of garlic bread off the plate in the center of the table, I take a large bite before setting the remains on the edge of my plate. The sound of clinking silverware on the plates is the only sound in the room as we eat. The silence is surprisingly comfortable.

'Sorry," I say after finishing over half of my meal. "I never answered your question," I say, pausing to take a drink of water. My shoulders sag in defeat. "We didn't find anything today, not that I expected to. Hoped to—definitely—find something," I say out loud, sagging back into my chair and heaving a heavy sigh.

"Tomorrow, we are starting at seven instead of eight. With luck, the extra hour of daylight will yield better results than today."

"Sorry that you didn't have a lot of luck today," Regina says softly. She seems like she has something on her mind. My eyes stay fixed on her face, waiting her out as we continue eating.

After several moments without her saying anything else, I broach the subject.

"What is on your mind?" I ask bluntly.

Her gaze meets mine, and she nibbles on her bottom lip in thought.

"You don't need to be shy," I tell her. "Say what you want."

Regina's shoulders sag in relief at my words.

"I spoke to both Rafferty and Emmalee today," she says, pausing again, almost as if she is waiting for me to get angry that she spoke to her best friend and brother.

"What is going on with both of them?" I question, keeping my tone casual.

"Emma is going to be here in about ten days, give or take. Raff is going through my stuff. He is going to pack clothes, more than anything, for Em to bring with her," Regina tells me as a smile spreads across her face. "Emma is determined to find a man here."

I suppress a groan. If word gets out to the single men in town, they will be lined around the corner to meet this girl. It will take me and all three of my brothers to watch over these two women—I just know it.

We finish eating in silence and then clean the kitchen together, falling into a smooth rhythm. As soon as we are done, Regina heads upstairs as I make sure the house is locked up. Upon entering the bedroom, I find Regina already in bed, eyes closed. Stripping down and tossing my clothes in the laundry basket, I get a quick shower before climbing into bed behind her.

The weight of the day and our lack of sleep last night has sleep claiming me almost immediately.

Chapter 30 - Regina

It's been a week since Chayce and I mated. It is still taking me a while to get used to that term. He and the alphas have been working tirelessly to find whoever this person is prowling around town and breaking into businesses. From the little he has told me, the thefts have continued, possibly increasing, in addition to an increase in the number of tracks in various sections of town. He gets up early and comes home late. Chayce keeps promising me that he will take me out for a nice dinner as soon as things settle down. By the time he gets home, he is just too exhausted to do anything but eat, shower, and go to bed.

We have fallen into an easy routine. We enjoy dinner every night, making conversation and getting to know each other.

The insurance company finally made it out and looked at my car, approving the repairs. Kyle, through Chayce, has let me know that as soon as the parts arrive, which should be about another two weeks, he will get my car fixed. Chayce never mentioned if they found any trackers Jaygon might have put on my vehicle. Afraid of what the answer might be, I never asked.

Rafferty has most of my apartment packed up. Telling my landlord a little white lie that I got transferred for work got me out of my lease with no penalties. Raff updates me every few days and has informed me that Jaygon is still missing. Rafferty also said there has been no activity on his bank accounts, credit cards, or cellphone. They aren't sure if he might be using a burner phone or what, but he is in the wind, practically disappearing off the face of the Earth.

Because of this, Chayce won't let me go anywhere alone. Just a trip to the grocery store requires a guard. Brady and Adyr have been working nights, alternating between them. Usually, if I need to go anywhere, one of them takes me.

My ringing cell phone snaps me out of my daydream. A smile crosses my face when I see it's Emmalee.

"Where are you?" I ask, a smile spreading broadly across my face.

She laughs as she answers, "Looking at a gazebo in the middle of some nowhere town."

"You're here!" I screech, jumping to my feet. No doubt I just broke her eardrum.

"Yes, just pulled into town," Emma says, a bit of awe in her voice. "Where are you?"

"I am at home," I tell her, a little disappointed that I can't give her a guided tour around Padston. "If you stay on Main Street, on the second block, on the right-hand side, is the Whiskey Genie. Park the car—I will be there as soon as I can get a ride," I tell her, my mind scrambling on who I can call. I start to rush around, pulling out some fresh clothes. Since I wasn't sure she would make it in today, I didn't bother to fix myself up after my shower.

"Okay, see you soon," she says, disconnecting the call.

Hanging up with Em and dialing Brady's number, I start primping myself.

"What's up, sister?" Brady asks cheerily. All of the guys have taken to calling me sister since Chayce officially announced our mating.

"Can you please come and get me?" I ask in my most persuasive voice. "I need to go to the Whiskey Genie."

Brady hesitates, "Uhm, why?" he questions, drawing out the word why.

"Emma just pulled into town. She is going to be using the apartment upstairs. I need to say hello and help her get settled," I explain. "I also need to get my stuff from her car," I add on for good measure. "*And have some girl time*," I say to myself, but not out loud, knowing that if he knows we are going *into* the Genie for drinks, his answer would be no.

"Have you told Chayce?" Brady asks, pissing me off now.

My movement halts, my anger getting the better of me.

"He is my mate, not my keeper," I seethe. "I am an adult and am not required to report to him at all hours of the day." My chest heaves by the time my tirade ends. Calming down a little, I add, "Besides, I don't want to bother him while they are still looking for the prowler."

"Fuck!" Brady exclaims, and I know that I have won this argument. "I will be there in ten."

He hangs up with no more comment. Flitting around our bedroom and bathroom, I scramble to get ready, excited to see my best friend.

Stepping inside the Whiskey Genie, it isn't a surprise to find that Em has attracted the attention of the few people there. Gypsy has her head tipped back in laughter at something she has said. Approaching the duo with Brady following as my shadow, I know the moment Emmalee spots me. Em jumps from her chair, meeting me halfway, wrapping her arms tightly around my body. We sway back and forth as we hug. Tears pool in my eyes as it occurs to me how alone I have really felt until now.

We separate, each climbing into a bar stool. Emma's eyes pop out of her head, letting me know she has spotted Brady. Her gaze is locked on him, and she takes him in from head to toe.

"Emmalee, this is Brady, one of Chayce's brothers. Brady, this is my best friend, Emmalee Martin," I wave my hand back and forth between the pair as I do introductions.

"Hell-o," she says in a sultry voice as she continues to gawk at Brady. Gypsy laughs at Emma's antics, shaking her head back and forth as she pours us drinks.

"I thought you were bad," Gypsy says, addressing me. "Your girl here is going to start a lot of fights around here," she continues with a smile. Gypsy reaches under the bar, pulling out a clipboard with a chart of some kind on it. At my questioning look, she holds her hand out. "It's a pool," she explains. "We don't have much to do around here, so we gamble on anything and everything we can. If you have a guy in mind, you can bet on that person. If you want to wager on the type of shifter, you can do that. Other things you can bet on—time of the first fight, who will be in the fight, the winner...you get my point," Gypsy says, her voice trailing off, letting me fill in the gaps.

Giving my friend a sidelong glance, a wicked smile comes over my face. Pulling a twenty from my pocket and handing it to Gypsy, I place my bet.

"Fight, one hour... Madox and Hoyt..." Emma's mouth is gaping open at me. "Mate, Jorden," I say with a smirk in Emma's direction. She gives me a raised eyebrow in response.

Gypsy writes it all down, laughing as she takes my money.

"Who is Jorden? Em asks because that is the most important part of the conversation.

Opening my mouth to answer, Gypsy beats me to it. "You'll see," she says to Emmalee, giving her a quick wink before moving down the bar to refill someone's glass.

Emmalee narrows her eyes at me, and I stick my tongue out at her in retaliation. Both of us end in a fit of laughs.

We have one drink before deciding that it's best to unload her car; if not, get Emma unpacked before we do anything else. Brady, bless him, helps with a lot of stuff. The handful of boxes that are mine he transferred into his truck to be taken home later.

Emma takes a quick shower, washing the road off herself. Putting the lid down, I sit on the toilet so we can talk as she gets ready. Nostalgia hits me, and I take a deep breath, letting it out slowly as I try to reign in my feelings. Heading back downstairs, Brady opens his mouth, but seeing my expression, he snaps it closed again without saying a word. Smart man. If Emmalee notices the exchange between the two of us, she doesn't comment.

Walking back into the Whiskey Genie, a lot of heads swing in our direction. It's more crowded inside the bar than it was just a little while ago. The hair on the back of my neck rises as a sense of unease washes over me. Trying to be covert, I only use my eyes to look around the room. Unfortunately, my presence in town has been too short for me to really see anything, or anyone, out of the ordinary. Maybe I can convince Chayce to have a party so I can meet more people.

"I know that look," Emmalee whispers. "What are you up to?" she asks, pausing to take a drink as she sits with her glass halfway to her mouth. Gypsy had our drinks waiting for us as we returned to the chairs we were in earlier.

"Something seems off, but I can't put my finger on it," I whisper. Emmalee starts to look around the room, but after a quick bump to her knee, with my own, she stops. "By the way, they all have enhanced hearing around here, so watch what you say and how loud you say it," I caution.

Emmalee's lips tip up on one side, letting me know she is saving that little tidbit for later. Despite not intending to, my words are like waving a red flag in front of a bull. Raising her glass in my direction in a silent salute, my head tilts back when I laugh.

"That sound is something a man could get used to hearing," a deep voice chimes in from behind me. My head whips to the side, finding Chayce standing there. Stepping closer, he wraps an arm around my shoulder while kissing the side of my head.

"Awwww, you guys are too cute," Emma says a little too loudly as she makes kissy faces and us.

Several people around us snicker at her words.

"Emmalee Monroe, this is Chayce Galloway, my mate. Chayce, this is my best friend in the universe, Emmalee."

The two of them exchange pleasantries as Gypsy hands Chayce a beer.

"Is it safe to assume that Brady told you we were here?" I ask Chayce as I shoot a glare at an unapologetic-looking Brady standing behind him. Chayce nods as he takes a pull off his beer.

"Yes," he answers, pausing before continuing to speak. "How long are you planning on staying?"

For some reason, his question, while innocent enough, has my dander up. My words are sharper than necessary, especially in a crowded bar full of people with advanced hearing.

"Until I am ready to leave," I bite out in response.

Gypsy breaks the tension building between us as she passes by us, dropping off beers and cocktails as she goes.

"You don't win the bet if *you* start the fight."

Both Emma and I break out into fits of laughter as Chayce's brown furrow. My shoulder sags, realizing what happened, making me feel like shit. Pulling the front of his shirt down, forcing our faces together, I whisper in his ear.

"I am sorry. Brady gave me a lecture earlier, making it sound as if I wasn't allowed to leave the house," I explain. "You hit a nerve."

Instead of responding with words, Chayce spins the barstool so I am facing him. Cradling my face with both hands, he leans in, giving me a sultry kiss that makes my cheeks heat and my panties wet. In true best friend fashion, Em starts clapping and cheering, causing the entire bar to get in on the act. When Chayce breaks the kiss, my forehead hits the middle of his chest, trying to hide my embarrassment.

"You are a troublemaker, aren't you?" Chayce asks Emmalee.

"What can I say?" she quips with a shrug. "I play to my strengths."

Now it's Chayce's turn to toss his head back in laughter. Gypsy approaches us, clipboard in hand. Waving it in the air, she taunts Chayce.

"Sheriff, do you want to place a bet?" she asks him, waving the clipboard in the air as she gives me a wink.

Dig's
DINER
READERS WORLD
BOOKS

Chapter 31 - Chayce

Once I made my presence known to Regina, I moved down the bar to give her and Emmalee some privacy. My girl is radiating happiness right now. My dragon huffs out a frustrated breath at not realizing she was down. No, that isn't the right word. I'm not sure what it is, but this is a side that I haven't seen, and I like it. Regina is carefree right now, just enjoying life. This situation of Jaygon must be weighing heavier on her than I thought.

"Sheriff, taking a night off?" a deep voice says to my left.

Looking over my shoulder, I find Tavan Russell standing there, a dark glass in his hand, the scent of blood strong.

"Hey Doc, how are you?" I ask, returning the greeting.

"Doing well," he answers. "Congratulations on your mating."

"Thank you. We are still settling in. This has been a big adjustment for Regina, moving to such a small town and all," I add on, not mentioning the threat from Jaygon looming over our heads.

Using his glass to indicate the spot where my girl and her friend are holding court, he smiles.

"Those two are going to be trouble together," he says with a chuckle, making me cringe.

Rubbing the back of my neck, something that is becoming a bad habit, I nod. He doesn't see it since he is watching the girls.

"Yeah, but Regina needed this," I comment, mostly to myself, since Tavan isn't paying attention.

"Oh, shit," he hisses.

My head whips around searching the room for a threat, trying to figure out what Tavan is talking about. It takes a minute since the bar is crowded. My dragon is at attention when I spot the issue.

The Martin triplets have approached Regina and Emmalee. The tension in the bar immediately ratchets up. These girls are predators and are known around town for being unforgiving when it comes to other women encroaching on their territory. An eerie silence has fallen over the crowd.

"I'm Roree Martin," the girl says. "These are my sisters Raelee and Rhodee."

That is all Roree says, and all three women stand with their arms across their chests, staring Emmalee and Regina down. Surprisingly, Emmalee breaks the tension like a hot knife through butter.

"Thank God!" she exclaims, clapping her hands together to emphasize her words. "More women, this place was becoming a total sausage fest."

Everyone in the bar holds their breath, waiting for the Martin girls to react. It takes a second before all five ladies start laughing. Gypsy hands the triplets beers, and all five girls move to the far corner to shoot some pool. A sharp slap to my back has my head whipping around.

"Breathe," Tavan says, all too amused.

Chugging the rest of my beer, Gypsy has a fresh bottle and a shot of something sitting in front of me.

"I think you are going to need that, Sheriff," she says, giving a nod toward the bar top.

I down the shot, pushing the empty glass across the bar along with my empty beer bottle.

It isn't long before that stupid clipboard starts getting passed around again as shouts from the girls fill the air.

Luckily, the evening passed without incident. Once the girls all started playing pool, guys started to approach them, checking out Emmalee. The Martin triplets actually kept the mayhem to a minimum. Many patrons were disappointed that a fight never broke out. Thankfully, Regina kept space between any approaching male and herself. My dragon spent the night on alert but never tried to break free.

It's late morning now, and Regina is still sleeping off last night. I should be out leading a search, but we decided to take a break.

There isn't much to do around the house since Regina has been picking up my slack. Brady dropped off the boxes that Emmalee brought this morning. Not knowing what is in them or where Regina wants anything, I move them to one of the spare bedrooms. She can sort through them at her leisure.

Hearing Regina move about upstairs, I work on getting her some breakfast. With the day off, spending some time alone is at the top of my priority list.

A few minutes later, a disheveled-looking Regina enters the kitchen. Wearing one of my T-shirts, her hair pulled up in a messy knot on top of her head, and her eyes half closed, she makes her way to the table. Letting out a soft chuckle, I set a fresh cup of coffee in front of her and return to the stove to finish cooking.

It doesn't take long for breakfast to be ready. After setting plates on the table, I sit, and we eat in companionable silence. As time passes, Regina looks more like herself.

"Did you have fun last night, baby?" I ask, keeping my voice just above a whisper in case she is hungover.

A soft smile graces Regina's lips.

"I did," she says, taking a sip of coffee. "Thank you."

"Why are you thanking me?" I question, confused by her statement.

"You worked all day; no doubt you were tired. Yet, you stayed and made sure Em and I were safe." Taking another sip of coffee, her words stop. When I think she is done speaking, she shocks me with her next statement. "While I love you, we still need to do our own thing so I don't smother you in your sleep," she says, making the last part sound questionable as to her being serious or joking.

"You love me?" I say, my breath stalling in my chest. Regina just dropped that statement as if she was talking about the weather, catching me off guard.

"Well, yeah," she shrugs, "You are kinda stuck with me now. We just can't lose who we are as individuals just because we are a couple," she says that last part softly.

Before realizing it, my body is now in front of her. Pulling her out of her chair, I lay her on the table, brushing anything that is in my way aside. I ignore the items that clatter to the floor, something breaking. Leaning over Regina's body, kissing her passionately, one of my claws extend, removing her panties from her body.

My fingers run through her folds, finding her wet for me. Teasing her clit with my thumb, two fingers slide easily into her channel. Planting kisses along her jawline and down her neck, my fingers continue to move in and out of her tight pussy.

Working kisses down the length of Regina's body, I pull one of her puckered nipples into my mouth through the shirt, leaving a wet spot. Kneeling down, my thumbs spread her folds open. Looking at the pink flesh, my cock pulses, remembering what it feels like to have her wrapped around my length.

Moving closer, I swipe my tongue from the bottom to the top of her slit. Regina's back bows off the table, writhing in pleasure. Taking her clit between my teeth, my fingers slide into her again, rubbing her outer wall.

"Chayce, yesssss," she says with a moan, her head thrashing back and forth.

Her hand reaches up, grabbing a fist full of hair, pulling me closer to her center. My fingers move harder and faster as I suck her clit, bringing her closer to climax.

Using my free hand to release my cock, I rise to my feet. As Regina opens her mouth to protest the loss of my mouth, I slam my cock inside her. She screams at the sudden intrusion, but it quickly turns into a moan as I fuck her. Pulling her upper body to a sitting position, I take her mouth in a punishing kiss as my hips continue to move. Regina wraps her legs around my waist and she reaches her peak. She moans into my mouth as a sudden rush of wetness coats my cock.

Working Regina through her orgasm as her pussy squeezes my dick, my fingers dig into the globes of her ass. My pace is brutal and unrelenting. Breaking the kiss and trailing more kisses along her jawline, I bite her earlobe. My voice is laced with lust and comes out with a hint of a growl. My dragon is close to the surface and wants to reclaim her.

"I want you to come again," I tell her. "I want to feel you milk my cock as we both come."

Regina opens her mouth, but the only thing that comes out is a moan. My claws extend, slicing her shirt out of the way, tearing through the material like a hot knife through butter. She gasps as the cooler air hits her heated flesh.

Snaking my hand between our bodies, I use my thumb to rub her clit. My orgasm is rapidly approaching and I want her to come with me. Regina tosses her head back on her shoulder and my teeth elongate at the sight of her long, slender neck exposed to me. Piercing the skin of her neck, on the opposite side from my mate mark, I rub hard on her clit. Her orgasm hits and her pussy grips my dick like a vice, pulling me over the edge with her. My hips slow, working both of us through our climaxes. My tongue snakes out, lapping up the traces of blood from my bite. She shudders at the sensation.

We stay like that, wrapped in each other's arms, as my hips still.

Disregarding the mess we made, I lift Regina off the table—maintaining our connection, I walk us upstairs and into the shower.

Chapter 32 - Regina

Chayce won't tell me what we are going today, only that I need to dress warm.

After he fucked me on the kitchen table, we had sex again in the shower. We were in there so long the hot water ran out. Apprehension took over this morning when I inadvertently blurted out those three little words. He didn't say them back, which is nerve-wracking, but he did show me how he felt. Still, it would be nice to hear them spoken.

Trying to brush away the disappointment and self-depreciation at jumping the gun, I finish getting dressed. Chayce seems nervous for some reason and it's making me nervous in return. Heading downstairs, I find him pacing the floor. My eyebrows crease as my footsteps falter, not sure of the reason. Immediately, the trespasser comes to mind.

"Has something happened?" I ask, a nervous edge to my tone.

"No," he responds, his words clipped, not giving me any reassurances on the matter.

"Yeah, okay," I say sarcastically, making my feelings known.

Trying to brush off whatever his issue is, I continue down the stairs, grabbing my purse and phone on the way to Chayce's truck. He rushes to catch up to me.

Riding in silence to our mystery destination, the tension between us is palpable. Unsure of where we are going or what we are doing, I break my silence, having had enough, after about twenty minutes.

"Chayce, what is going on?" I ask, my tone sharp.

"I...I," he stutters, saying nothing more.

Drumming his fingers on the steering wheel, he turns the truck onto a side road that doesn't appear to have been used since the snow hit. Putting the truck into park in the middle of a large clearing, Chayce turns to face me.

"I want to show you my dragon," he says nervously.

A smile blooms across my face as excitement fills me.

"Really?" I ask, surprised.

Feeling giddy, I start to bounce around in my seat. I thought he had forgotten about me asking. Taking my hands in his, Chayce speaks, his words gentle.

"I love you, Regina."

A calm washes over my body as an invisible weight floats away at his declaration.

I start to launch myself into his arms, only to get caught up by the seatbelt. We both laugh as I fumble to get it released. As soon as my body is released, I move without thought into his arms. Our lips find each other, and it isn't long before clothes start coming off.

Chayce lays me down across the bench seat of his truck and slowly makes love to me. It is a bit uncomfortable in a confined space, but that doesn't matter.

After helping me clean up as best as we can since having a quickie in the middle of nowhere was not on my radar, I get dressed. Chayce looks nervous again. Squeezing his hand, my words are soft and reassuring.

"If you don't want to do this, we don't have to."

Taking a deep breath, letting it out slowly, he gives me a quick nod before opening the truck door. Standing bare ass naked in the cold and snow, I rush to climb from the truck, grabbing his coat as I go. Rounding the front of the truck, Chayce gives me a quick, chaste kiss before walking off.

The air around Chayce seems to shimmer and my excitement is a living, breathing thing. Slowly, his body contorts and grows. After what seems like an hour but is actually mere seconds, a massive dark orange dragon looms before me. His neck and snout extend into the air as a large flame shoots from his mouth. It is easy to feel the heat from here. Unlike Chayce's brown eyes, his dragons are a bright emerald green. They appear brighter, offset by the orange.

Taking slow, measured steps, I approach him, not sure how much of Chayce is present compared to the mind of his dragon. He lowers his head, melting the snow under him from the heat he is radiating. Stepping up next to him, my hand reaches out to touch him.

His scales feel different than expected. They are cool to the touch, thin, but not brittle. They come to a point, the shape similar to a guitar pick. Running my fingers up his long nose, smoke billows from his snout. My body lurches, falling against Chayce for support. When I look over my shoulder, his tail catches my attention.

His tail is long, slimming out as it gets farther away from his body. The end has sharp-looking barbs that no doubt can do a lot of damage if he is angry. My face hurts from smiling so much, a semi-permanent grin frozen in place. Giving him an awkward hug, he growls in approval.

"You are exquisite!"

Chayce suddenly moves to stand on his hind legs, once again blowing fire up into the sky.

I retrace my steps through the deep snow back to the truck as Chayce's dragon retreats, giving him back his human form. Walking through the mud, he finds an untouched section of snow and uses it to clean up.

"One of the hazards of my fire," he says flatly in explanation. "Climb back in—we will go eat." Chayce starts to get dressed, and I walk around the other side and climb in, leaning sideways to turn the key and get some heat going. Once he is dressed, he gets behind the wheel and points the truck toward town. My stomach is rumbling as we park in front of the steakhouse. Stepping out of the truck, the smell of seared meat floats through the air. Simmer Down is painted on the sign that runs along the roofline.

"The bears own this place," Chayce whispers. "Fair warning, the portions are large. I hope you are hungry." He holds the door open for me to step inside.

The Western-style theme fits somehow. This entire town, in fact, seems like it could easily be located in the Old West. One of the triplets greets us from the hostess stand. Since they are identical, I have no idea which one it is. Instead of embarrassing myself by calling her the wrong name, which no doubt happens often, I keep my greeting to a simple "hi." She grabs two menus and some wrapped silverware, leading us to a booth in the far corner.

Since showing me his dragon, Chayce is much more relaxed, and our conversation flows easily.

Our first official "date" was perfect.

Dig's
DINER
READERS WORLD

Chapter 33 - Chayce

Regina's reaction to my dragon was better than I could have hoped for. Finally, being able to take her out for a date was the cherry on top of the proverbial sundae.

Driving us home, I catch Regina twisting her fingers, a nervous gesture I have picked up on.

"Whatever you want to say, just say it, please," I blurt out, wanting to get the conversation started. "You are going to hurt yourself the way you are twitching," I add, trying to soften my criticism.

"I want to have a party," she states nervously.

"Okay," I say, drawing out the word, expecting more details. "Are you expecting me to say no?" I ask, wanting her to feel comfortable and not feel like she needs to ask permission.

"Hear me out before you freak out," she says, causing the hair on the back of my neck to rise.

She heaves a heavy sigh as she continues, "Yesterday, at the Whiskey Genie when Emma and I first got there, something was bothering me. It was as if I was being watched."

"What?!" I cut her off as anger explodes in my chest and smoke spills from my nose. "Why didn't you say something then? Where was Brady?" My questions come rapid-fire, not giving her a chance to answer in between them.

"Calm down," she huffs out. "Brady was right behind me," Regina says, waving me off. "Looking around to see who it might have been was useless. It occurred to me I don't know many people here. It was a total waste of time to search for an unfamiliar face, as they are *all* unfamiliar," Regina says.

"Fuck. That never occurred to me," I say, my shoulders sagging in frustration.

Showing her around town and introducing her is now one of my main goals.

"Okay, plan your party. Where do you want to have it?" I concede, trying to think of a location.

"I would like to have it at the house if you don't mind?" Biting her lip, she worries her fingers together even more in anticipation of my response. "Would you mind if Em stayed in one of the spare rooms so she doesn't have to worry about driving?" she asks so quickly that all of the words seem to run together. It takes me a moment to make sense of her question.

"We can do whatever you want," I tell her, only wanting to make her happy. "However and wherever you want to do it." Regina bounces in her seat, clapping her hands in excitement. "I am sorry. It never occurred to me that other than the alphas and my brothers, you haven't met many people."

"Speaking of alphas," she interrupts. "Would you mind asking them to come? Bring some people from their groups, or packs, or herds, whatever they are called," Regina says, causing me to laugh.

She narrows her eyes at me due to my laughter. Holding up a hand in surrender, she sags back in her seat.

"It was your general term that had me chuckling," I explain. "Lions live in a pride. Bears live in a den. Wolves live in a pack. It's how we refer to the various sections of town." I watch her facial expressions with each new bit of information about her new home. "For the most part, the various shifter types live together."

"Oh," she says with a relieved huff. "I need to call the triplets and invite them."

Suppressing a groan at the mention of the Martin triplets, my stomach clenches at her making friends with the town troublemakers. They are good, decent girls who get bored easily, especially when they are together. My lips tip up on one side as thoughts of the poor saps who get stuck with one of them. They are in for a fight.

Arriving at home, as soon as Regina gets settled, she starts making phone calls for this party. What I expected to be a quiet night at home is now a party planning session. Planting my ass on the couch, beer in one hand, remote in the other, a soft smile crosses my face at the happiness in Regina's voice.

I wouldn't have it any other way.

Chapter 34 - Regina

This week has flown by.

The triplets have been a massive help in recommending who to invite. Chayce reached out to the alphas, and we are expecting around fifty people. I am not sure who is more excited about this. Me, as it will give me a chance to meet Chayce's friends and hopefully make some of my own. Emmalee, since she will be able to meet more of the single men in town since she is still on the hunt, so to speak. Possibly, the triplets, since they have managed to get a Saturday night off all at once.

I am thankful that my job offers me the freedom to set my own hours. If not, I would be pulling my hair out, worried about tonight. Emmalee has helped me with the shopping and other planning since she doesn't have much to do with herself at the moment.

Chayce and the other men in town are still going out daily in search of the person breaking into the businesses. It is frustrating to them all how this person is remaining under the radar.

Wanting to look nice, I pull out a peach-colored sweater dress, matching it with a pair of brown suede boots that come up over my knee. Leaving my hair down, styled with soft curls, and keeping my makeup neutral, I am happy with the look.

The bedroom door opens, and Chayce lets out a growl when he sees me, smoke escaping from his nose.

"You need to change that outfit," he orders, causing my brows to furrow.

Looking down at my body, my hands smooth out the material. Checking the mirror, my eyes meet his in the reflection.

Not seeing what is wrong, I turn to face him, finding him right in front of me. Damn shifter speed.

"What is wrong with my outfit?" I bark. "I thought it looked nice."

"It does," he clips out. "Too nice. These assholes don't need to see you like this. Put on a sack, or better yet, put on a pair of my sweatpants and a sweatshirt," Chayce says, turning to the dresser where he starts pulling those garments out. "These will keep you covered up." He extends the articles of clothing in my direction.

How he manages to say all of this with a straight face is beyond me. Laughing at him, I pat his chest as I pass him on my way to the door.

"You are ridiculous," I say over my shoulder.

His grumbled reply is muted as the door closes behind me. My head shakes from side to side at his antics, and a large smile spreads across my face. Emmalee steps out of the spare room at the same time I step into the hall. She gives me a questioning look. Waving it off, we head downstairs to start putting the food out.

The party is in full swing.

There are more people here than expected, but who cares. Em has had more male attention than she knows what to do with. Several times, I have caught Jorden eying her, a scowl planted firmly on his face. One side of my mouth quirks up at that. He is the one I picked for her and is also the one who will win me the pool at the bar.

It is cold enough outside that most of the beer, bottles of water, and cans of soda are there. We didn't have to worry about coolers or ice with all the snow around. Someone got creative and put the individual bottles directly into the snow.

Taking a moment to step outside for some fresh air, the temperature difference is extreme. With all of the higher-than-normal body temperatures in the house, multiplied by the number of people, I am starting to sweat.

The sliding glass door opens behind me, and Chayce steps out.

"Are you okay?" he questions.

"I am fine. It was getting too hot in there. I just needed a minute to cool down," I reassure him.

Chayce wraps his arms around me, kissing me softly.

"Your party is a success," he quips before his tone turns serious. "Are you happy, love?"

"I am," I tell him sincerely. "Thank you for letting me do this."

We hold each other for several minutes, just taking a moment to ourselves. Unfortunately, it doesn't last long as Adyr sticks his head out the door, calling for Chayce.

"Will you be okay out here alone?" Chayce asks, his eyes doing a quick scan of the dark backyard.

Planting a soft kiss on my lips, Chayce heads back inside, trailing after his brother.

Opening a bottle of water and staring out into the woods, my thoughts drift to how much my life has changed for the better in such a short period of time. Emmalee is happy here, but she isn't staying.

A sound comes from behind me, but before I can turn around, a hand moves over my mouth, muffling my cries.

"It's about time you are alone."

That is the last thing I hear before my world goes dark.

Dig's
DINER
READERS WORLD
CARDS
BOOKS

Chapter 35 - Chayce

This party has been a lot of fun and I need to make sure Regina knows it. We all needed this. Frustration has grown over our inability to find this person terrorizing our small town.

When Adyr called me away from Regina, I loathed having to separate from her. She needs her space and can't have me hovering all the time, and it's something I have to remind myself of often. It has taken a lot to let her go tonight. Knowing that she is safe in our home is the only thing that has kept me sane. That and being surrounded by so many friends and predators.

The crowd is starting to thin, finally. Roree, Raelee, and Rhodee are walking around picking up empty plates and bottles, helping to clean up. Emmalee is in the kitchen washing dishes and putting food away. It's then that my blood runs cold as it occurs to me that Regina is nowhere in sight. An uneasiness creeps up my spine. Approaching the girls, I stumble over my words, fearing the worst.

"Have any of you seen Regina lately?"

Our remaining guests all stop whatever conversations they are in the middle of. Everyone is now focused on me. One by one, as my gaze meets each of theirs, a shake of the head brings my greatest fear to life.

My dragon pushes to the surface, causing Emmalee's eyes to widen as smoke billows from my nose and mouth. Taking the stairs two at a time to make sure she hadn't just fallen asleep or passed out, each room gets thoroughly checked.

Confirming her absence on the second floor, I repeat my action, moving room by room on the first floor. Still unable to find her, I step outside. On the patio, where I saw her last, is a water bottle. It's lying on its side on the concrete, a small puddle underneath it on the ground.

This time, my dragon does break loose, my clothes shredding. My fire lights up the sky as my wings lift me into the air.

Doing several loops around the surrounding area does nothing to calm me down. There is no trace or sign of Regina. I am more angry now than before I took flight after realizing she is missing.

Returning to the house, a pile of clothes is sitting there, waiting for me. Pulling them on, I step inside. All of the alphas are here, along with several betas and hunters, as well as my brothers.

"Has anyone seen my phone?" I call out, having lost track of it.

Deakon pulls his phone out, and a few seconds later, a ringing can be heard coming from upstairs. Sprinting to grab it and scrolling through my contacts, I connect the call I never expected to make.

"Yeah," the sleepy voice answers. A glance at the clock tells me it's after midnight. Without a preamble, my voice is harsh as my dragon bleeds through.

"Have you located Jaygon Jones yet?" I bite out, misdirecting my anger at Rafferty.

"No, why?" He is wide awake now, and I have his full attention.

"Regina is missing."

"What. The. Fuck. Do. You. Mean. Missing?" Rafferty bites out every word, and he has every right to be pissed.

"We had a party tonight, so she and Emmalee could meet some of the townspeople," I tell him with the briefest of explanations. "Last week, Regina said that she felt like someone was watching her. Not knowing anyone, she was unable to identify it there was a real cause for alarm."

"Where the fuck were you during this party?" he sneers.

"Do *not* go there," I say in warning. "I have already been out searching and can find no trace of her."

"Fuck," he heaves out. "All right, let me make some calls. Keep your phone handy, and keep me updated on Regina."

Rafferty hangs up, not saying another word.

Moving back to the living room, all eyes are on me. Approaching my friends, I review the conversation with Rafferty Chaney.

"My wolves are already on the move," Crispin says.

"Looking over our grid map, this area hasn't been checked yet in our search for our thief. Jaygon could be hiding in an unknown cave," Deakon says, looking at the map on his phone.

The safe thing to do is wait until morning to start our search when it's daylight. Crispin's wolves have Regina's scent, so it should be pretty easy to catch up with her and Jones. That's assuming it's him and not one of the people he has contracts with who have her.

Mentally running through every face that I saw tonight, no unknown sticks out.

"Did any of you see anyone strange tonight?" I ask, voicing my thoughts in case our kidnapper is avoiding me. "This town isn't that big."

The group shakes their head "no" at my question. Jorden surprises everyone when he points at Emmalee.

"What about her?" he says accusatorily.

Hurt crosses her face before a mask of anger takes over. Marching over to stand in front of Jorden, she pokes him in the chest with each word as she tries to hold back tears.

"If you think for one fucking moment that I have anything to do with this, you are out of your mind. That girl is like a sister to me and I would rather cut my arm off than see anything bad happen to her," Emmalee seethes. "I hate Jaygon Jones with a passion. The guy is a snake. When G met him, I told her he was no good. She tried to give him the benefit of the doubt because she is too fuckin' nice." By the time her rant is over, Emmalee's chest is heaving as tears stream down her cheeks.

The triplets pull her into a group hug, glaring at Jorden. Jorden storms outside, slamming the door closed behind him in frustration.

Suddenly “Bitch” by Meredith Brooks starts playing, drawing confused looks. Emmalee is a flurry of activity as she fumbles with her cell phone, struggling to get it out of her pocket.

“Regina...” she asks hopefully, as everyone’s attention is focused on Emmalee.

“Em...help,” is all she gets out before the line goes dead and the room erupts into total chaos.

Chapter 36 - Regina

It's so incredibly cold.

My body is shaking, my teeth chattering from the lack of heat. A drip, drip, drip sounds in the distance through the ringing in my ears and pounding in my head. The darkness is a living, breathing entity.

The last thing I remember is a voice whispering in my ear as my mouth was being covered, smothering any sounds I might have made.

Wherever they have brought me is not conducive for living. Both the floor and the walls are rough, hard, cold, and wet. Outside of the consistent dripping, the only other sounds are the beating of my heart and my breathing.

Crawling around on my hands and knees, since I don't know how high the ceiling might be, my hands wave around finding nothing around me but hard rock. Leaning against the wall and wrapping my arms around me to try and keep warm, my hands brush against something hard. Frantically feeling around my body, I almost cry in relief, finding my phone.

If I am being watched somehow, the brightness of the screen is going to give me away. It is a risk I am going to have to take.

Quickly unlocking the screen, I pull up the last person called. It just happens to be Em. Just before the call goes to voicemail, she answers in a shaky voice.

"Regina..." she says hopefully.

"Em...help," that is all I get out before my phone is ripped away. The sound of it breaking, as if smashed against the rocks, breaks my heart.

My head whips to the side as a sharp slap to the face startles me.

“Stupid girl,” is all they say before the world goes dark again.

Dig's
DINER
READERS WORLD

Chapter 37 - Chayce

We have tried everything to pinpoint Regina's location. Deakon was able to get a general area, which helps, but it's not enough. She is in an area that we haven't had a chance to search yet, and it's large. I guess Jaygon was taking advantage of our situation.

The sun is finally starting to rise. Almost the entire town has turned out to help find my mate.

Climbing into my truck, my brothers in tow, my phone rings. Starting it up, the phone kicks to the hands-free system built into the radio.

"It's not Jaygon Jones that has Gina," the deep voice that is becoming all too familiar says.

If the truck was moving, I would have slammed on the brakes at Rafferty's statement.

"What do you mean it's not Jaygon?" Adyr asks for me. I ignore the fact that he climbed into the truck without me noticing, my mind too distracted to comprehend what this means. Being up for twenty-four hours will do that, I guess.

"Jaygon Jones's body was found this morning. His head was removed," Rafferty says flatly.

"Well, if it isn't him, that means one of the guys looking for payment has her," Brady interjects. When did he get here? Shaking my head to clear the random thoughts popping into my head, I focus back on the conversation with Rafferty.

"There was a note with the body. The long and short of it is that they have no interest in Gina," he says.

"What. The. Fuck?" Brady says, taking the words out of my mouth.

"Exactly," Rafferty says with a huff. "So if it isn't Jaygon and his business partners, for lack of a better term, aren't behind this, who the fuck is?" he asks angrily.

"Regina was able to call Emmalee last night. The call got disconnected, but we have been able to narrow down the area the call originated from. We are on our way there now. Our doctor is on standby in case she needs medical attention." Adyr gives Rafferty the information, leaving me to process all of this new information.

"Okay, go find our girl," Rafferty orders, adding on, "keep me updated on what's going on."

He and Adyr talk a little more, but it all fades into the background.

Chapter 38 - Regina

Trying to open my eyes, my body is too sluggish to respond. At some point, my hands have been tied behind my back. The cold seeping into my bones is making my entire body ache. Unable to keep my head up, I use the unforgiving wall behind me to support the heavy weight.

A rough voice speaks, echoing through the room I am being held in.

"Your mate couldn't just leave well enough alone, could he?" the echo makes my head pound harder than it already is.

"Wh-wha-what…a-a-are…y-you…ta-ta-talk-ing…ab-about?" I stutter out between chattering teeth.

"ME!" they scream out, causing me to flinch. "I just needed some supplies to get through the cold and to heal. He couldn't just leave me alone. Do you know how many times he has almost caught me? DO YOU?"

Unable to answer or understand what they are talking about, my head tilts to the side. Finding it difficult to keep my eyes open, my body relaxes as the shaking starts to subside. A soft smile crosses my lips as the ground shakes and a loud roar sounds.

"Chayce…" my whisper is the last thing I remember.

Dig's
DINER
READERS WORLD

Chapter 39 - Chayce

We are in the same clearing Regina and I were in when I showed her my dragon. Ours were the only tracks at the time. As soon as I realized where we were, my dragon took over, flying in low, slow circles. As soon as I caught her faint scent, we flew back to tell the others.

Immediately, we turned our focus onto that area.

We find a cave entrance hidden under a curtain of moss, leaves, and branches. For a brief moment, I wonder how many other places similar to this we overlooked. Pushing the thought aside, Regina's scent assaults me from multiple directions.

A hand on my shoulder has my head spinning around, snapping my neck in the process.

Adyr holds his hands up, taking a step back before speaking.

"Calm yourself," he says softly. "You are her mate. If you settle your mind, you should be able to hear her heartbeat and smell her. Release your dragon. Let him help you."

Closing my eyes and relaxing my body, I let go, giving my dragon control without the shift. It's an odd sensation and something we haven't tried before. Breathing deeply and quieting my mind, a very faint heartbeat is detected. It is actually starting to slow down. Moving my arms out to the side, I strike walls on both sides of me, letting out an angry roar.

My feet start moving, racing to find her. Knowing my brothers are following me, I concentrate on Regina, letting them deal with the threat. After what seems like an eternity, the cave opens into a large room. A small figure is on the far side as Regina is slumped on the floor in front of me.

Leaving my brothers to deal with this unknown person, I pick up Regina's limp form and run back to the cave's entrance. As soon as possible, my dragon takes form, taking to the sky. My chest heats, trying to warm Regina's body.

In no time at all, I am landing in the street in front of Tavan's clinic. I change back to human form as quickly as I changed to my dragon. Rushing inside, Tavan guides me into one of his exam rooms.

"There are scrubs in the corner," he says offhandedly, his focus on my mate. "Something there should fit you." Tavan gives me instructions while tending to Regina. "If you can behave and be quiet, you can stay," he says in warning. "If no, go sit in the waiting room."

Finding it best not to comment, I get dressed then flop into a chair, sitting on my hands, my eyes never leaving Regina. Tavan hooks her up to an IV and covers her in hot water bottles and blankets.

"She is dehydrated and has mild hypothermia. Other than that, she seems to be okay," he says, and a rush of breath escapes my lungs in relief. "I need you to climb up on her other side," Tavan says, indicating the side opposite where the IV line is in her arm. "Your body heat can help warm her faster."

Tavan barely finishes his statement, and I am lying next to her, pulling her body tightly against mine on the small exam table.

"Just stay like that. I will be back to check on you in a little while," he orders before leaving the room.

Having Regina in my arms has me relaxing slightly. The unknown person in that cave is something that needs to be handled, but it can wait until tomorrow. My eyes drift closed, and at some point, I fall asleep.

Hearing a throat clear has my eyes popping back open. My brothers are standing just inside the door, watching us. Glancing down at Regina's face, her eyes are still closed, her breathing steady.

"The person from the cave is secure in the jail. Crispin, Jorden, and Madox have offered to watch her," Adyr whispers so as not to disturb my girl. "We wanted to come and check on you both."

"Can you please call Rafferty? Oh, and Emmalee? Let them know we found her?" I ask, my mind running on overdrive and switching from concerned mate to Sheriff.

"It's already been handled. Rafferty asked that one or both of you call him later on, tomorrow at the latest," Brady adds.

Regina stirs, causing all of us to go still.

Tavan enters the room, giving my brothers a resigned look. "I understand, but get out," he says flatly. Not wanting to argue, they start to leave. Just before Tavan closes the door, Deakon pushes it back open, setting my cell phone on the chair next to the door.

Tavan checks Regina's IV, adding another bag of fluids and then another blanket over both of us. It's too hot for me, but I ignore it.

"Once she wakes up, and I can do a full exam, she should be able to go home," he tells me. My shoulders sag in relief.

Nodding in lieu of an answer, he leaves again. My chest heats, hoping to speed up the process.

Chapter 40 - Regina

Hot.

What is going on?

First, I was freezing, and now I am sweating my ass off. Trying to push off the covers is a waste of time. It isn't until my brain registers Chayce wrapped around me like a spider monkey that I realize I am safe.

Peering up, our eyes lock. Without thought, we kiss. It is all-consuming, as if we say a hundred things in that one act.

"Welcome back, love," he barely manages to get out. "We thought we lost you."

Before getting a chance to ask questions or comment, the door opens. Looking over my shoulder, the doctor has a soft smile on his face as he enters.

"Chayce, if you would please step out of the room? We shouldn't be long," he says as he starts gathering supplies.

Chayce hesitates, which, given the situation, is understandable.

"She will be fine," Doctor Russell assures him. "I just need to check a few things and you can take her home."

Begrudgingly, Chayce gets up and leaves the room.

The doctor asks me several questions about how I am feeling as well as performing some range of motion tests. He gives me some instructions to follow over the next several days, advising me to call his office if anything feels off. Once he has finished checking me out, he tells me that I am free to go.

Startling at the sight of Chayce standing in the hallway, the doctor chuckles from behind me.

He takes a step toward me and sweeps me up into his arms, carrying me to the lobby. He wraps me up in a heavy coat before picking me back up and walking me outside to his truck. Chayce starts the truck and drives us home, holding my hand like it's a lifeline the entire way.

Dig's
DINER
READERS WORLD
CARDS
BOOKS

Chapter 41 - Chayce

It has been three days since we found Regina in that cave. She never seems to be warm enough. My girl has taken to wearing heavy, thick socks, sweatpants, long-sleeved shirts, and a sweatshirt. If I am home, she burrows into my chest as my dragon generates the heat she craves.

Needing to interrogate our kidnapper, Crispin, Adyr, Deakon, and Arek are at my house acting as security. Is it overkill? Probably. Do I care? Definitely not. Emmalee hasn't left my girl's side either. She has been cooking meals and waiting on her hand and foot.

With Brady at my side, we enter the section of the jail where the cells are. These cells are special since they typically house paranormals. When the jail was built, a traveling warlock bespelled them for us, negating the other side of ourselves when enclosed within, regardless of paranormal species.

Spinning a chair around to straddle it, my arms rest on the top of the back as I sit in front of the cell door.

"My name is Sheriff Galloway," I state flatly.

"Well aware of who you are, Sheriff," she spits out.

"What is your name?" I ask.

She says nothing, looking at the floor.

"Why are you in our town?"

Again, she refuses to answer.

"Why did you steal from us?"

Still, no answer. I wait her out a few more minutes before giving up. Nodding my head in silent response, I stand, put the chair back against the wall, and walk out.

Epilogue - Regina

It took two weeks for Chayce to finally get answers out of the woman who kidnapped me and stole from the town. Her name is Olivia, and she is a witch. She combined the footprints of three different animals to disguise her own tracks. Using a scent-masking spell, she hid herself.

The woman was escaping someone who wanted to harm her because she was a witch. She was able to evade them but had gotten hurt in the exchange. Her original plan was to continue to the coast. That isn't going to happen as she is awaiting charges and facing jail time, adding kidnapping to the trespassing and theft charges.

Emmalee went back to Boston last week. Something happened to my friend, and the light that shines from her soul is diminished.

Kyle finished my car, and Chayce and Brady went and picked it up. Home has become my refuge, as my anxiety spikes if I have to leave. The only way I go out is if Chayce is plastered to my side.

It is something that I need to work on, but not today.

Life has a way of steering our path to what will make us happy, even if we don't see it at the time. Like they say... when life gives you lemons, grab the tequila and make margaritas.

The End

About the author

I am a long-time reader turned author.

Some of my hobbies include camping, riding motorcycles, reading, collecting gnomes, and various crafts.

I live in Pennsylvania with my husband and three fur-babies.

Make sure you follow me everywhere and stay updated on all things bookish.

https://linktr.ee/annedwardsauthor

Acknowledgements

Thank you Kelly Jean, Cassie, and Ashley for your input and guidance.

Also by

Havoc Predators MC
The Daemon's Hacker
The Dragon's Barista
The Gargoyle's Wedding Planner
The Fae's Interpreter
The Griffin's Moviestar
The Goblin's Girlfriend
The Vampire's Waitress

Perpetual Fantasy Rock Band
Tanner
Zayn
Niall
Lorenzo
Austin
Stone (Coming Soon)

Groveton College Series (also available on Audio)
Hazing Her
Out of His League

Shifters of Padston
Swapped at the Altar
Hog Heaven (coming soon)

Shifters of Padston Companion Story
Mechanic

Havoc Predators MC, Baton Rouge

Voodoo Plantation (coming soon)

www.ingramcontent.com/pod-product-compliance
Lightning Source LLC
LaVergne TN
LVHW010547160826
845677LV00013B/3027

* 9 7 9 8 2 2 7 0 3 5 9 1 2 *